Dawson: He didn't think Joey would be so quick to agree that they should take things slowly. He wants her to have a good time in New York . . . just not too good a time.

Joey: She didn't really want to go to New York with Jen because she thought she'd be out of her league. But sophisticated senior Danny Fields has his eye on this small-town girl.

Pacey: He's busting to break away from his family—from Capeside. He's ready to hit the road. His father won't mind if he borrows the truck. Really.

Jen: She needs a Dawson-free zone now, and to her surprise, it's fun to be back with her old crowd in the big city—until ex-boyfriend Billy shows up.

DAWSON'S CREEK™

Don't miss any of these
Dawson's Creek™ books
featuring your favorite characters!

Dawson's Creek™ The Beginning of Everything Else
*A Novelization based on the hit television show
produced by Columbia TriStar Television.*

• More new, original stories featuring your favorite characters
from *Dawson's Creek*™, the hit television show:

LONG HOT SUMMER
CALM BEFORE THE STORM
SHIFTING INTO OVERDRIVE
MAJOR MELTDOWN
DOUBLE EXPOSURE

And don't miss:

• **Dawson's Creek**™ The Official Scrapbook

• **Dawson's Creek**™ The Official Postcard Book

Available now from Pocket Books.

Visit Pocket Books on the World Wide Web
http://www.SimonSays.com

Visit the Sony website at
http://www.dawsonscreek.com

Dawson's Creek™

Shifting Into Overdrive

Based on the television series "Dawson's Creek™"
created by **Kevin Williamson**

Written by C. J. Anders

POCKET BOOKS
New York London Toronto Sydney Tokyo Singapore

This book is a work of fiction. Names, characters, places and incidents are products of the author's imagination or are used fictitiously. Any resemblance to actual events or locales or persons living or dead is entirely coincidental.

An *Original* Publication of POCKET BOOKS

POCKET BOOKS, a division of Simon & Schuster Inc.
1230 Avenue of the Americas, New York, NY 10020

ISBN: 0-671-02476-0

First Pocket Books printing December 1998

10 9 8 7 6 5 4 3 2

POCKET and colophon are registered trademarks of Simon & Schuster Inc.

DAWSON'S CREEK is a registered trademark of Columbia TriStar Television, Inc.

Printed in the U.S.A.

—for Claire G., teen diva—

Chapter 1

Dawson Leery lay with his head against the pillows and frowned as he watched the end of *Thelma and Louise* on videotape, gazing at the TV against the wall.

"I ask you, Joey," he said, as the credits began to roll, "what point was the filmmaker trying to make with this cop-out ending? I mean, two women who've just pillaged their way across the country decide to run their car off a cliff with themselves in it? Which means . . . ?"

"No one but you cares what it means," his best friend, Josephine—better known as Joey—Potter stated, from her spot next to him on his bed. "And they didn't pillage, Dawson. They plundered. They plundered idiotic men who deserved to be plundered."

"And they murdered," Dawson added.

"Oh well, that," Joey said breezily.

"So why do girls love this movie?" Dawson asked. "It gives the illusion of depth when really it—"

"I hate to break this to you, Dawson, since I know how fragile your psyche is. But the reason we love this movie is not because of its quasi-feminist bent or nihilistic ending. I can sum it up for you in two words, Dawson, and those two words are: Brad Pitt."

Joey made a grab for the remote and reran the movie until she found the scene of Brad Pitt kissing Geena Davis. "Now *this* is art." She settled back against the pillows.

"But he's a drifter who rips her off!" Dawson protested. "What about romance?"

"What about those lips?" Joey replied.

A flush of irritation crept up the back of Dawson's neck. How did she expect him to feel when she talked like that? True, they'd been best friends forever and had only been a couple for, well, it had felt like minutes, until Joey had decided that being a couple wasn't what she really wanted at all.

Of course, that had happened just when Dawson finally decided that being a couple was exactly what *he* wanted. Why couldn't they ever both be in friendship mode or relationship mode at the same time?

"This part is great," Joey said, watching the screen. "This is where Brad—"

Dawson grabbed the remote from her.

"Hey!" Joey protested, lunging for it.

2

Dawson held it away from her. "Say 'Good night, Brad.'"

"Not until I *want* to say 'Good night, Brad.'" She scrambled over Dawson's stomach to get the remote. He began to tickle her, she punched him in the bicep, and he pushed her over until, before he knew it, he was lying on top of her, gazing down into those huge brown eyes of hers.

The fire was there. Incendiary. Not a "best friends" thing.

But did she feel it, too? "Joe?" he whispered.

Silence. She stared up at him.

So she *did* feel it! Slowly, his mouth came down, and—

"This is what is commonly called a compromising position," Joey said. "And best friends don't compromise."

He rolled off of her, beyond embarrassed.

"Well, was it good for you?" Joey quipped, trying to ease the tension. "If I smoked, I'd light a cigarette."

Dawson stared up at the ceiling. "The story arc of our movie is seriously flawed, Joe. Our act one was endless. Our act two lasted a nanosecond yet changed everything. And now there seems to be some confusion over whether we are to acknowledge that act two happened at all."

Joey pushed some hair away from her eyes. "It happened," she said. "We've just gone back to act one."

His eyes slid over to her. "In my admittedly limited experience, once you've experienced act two—

3

brief as it might have been—you can't go back to act one."

Joey sat up. "Sure you can. Just press rewind."

She knew exactly what Dawson meant, but at the moment, she didn't *want* to know. For so long it seemed as if all her time and energy had gone into wanting him. It wasn't that she didn't still have those feelings for him, because she did. But now . . . well, now she wanted the time and energy for something else. Maybe even *someone* else.

Dawson sat up, too. "I think it would benefit the everchanging nature of our relationship to discuss this."

"I think not," Joey replied. "Where's the remote?"

"I think so," Dawson insisted. He clicked off *Thelma and Louise*. "The delicate balance of us, whatever that may or may not be, dictates that—"

"We've talked it to death, Dawson," Joey said. "Let's give it a funeral and let it rest in peace."

Dawson shook his head. "That is not the most productive course of action. What would be helpful is—"

Joey made a noise of impatience under her breath. He could be so infuriating! "Let me ask you a question, Dawson, and feel free to answer it in twenty-five words or less because I'd hate to find myself experiencing middle-age spread with you still pondering this: Who made you writer, director, and star of this little drama?"

"We could share credit. I think the Directors Guild allows that," Dawson said. "Two equals who are—"

"Equals?" she interrupted. "All last year you called the shots. That is not what I call equal."

"I didn't mean to call the shots," Dawson said.

Joey shot him a dubious look.

"The salient point here is, I can change."

"No, you can't," Joey said. "I know you better than you know yourself, Dawson. It's easy for you to want me when I don't want you. No pressure there. But deep down your ambivalence about us is just as ambivalent as ever." She got up and grabbed her jacket.

"Where are you going?" he called to her.

"She gives him the big kiss off, fade to black." Joey headed for the window, her usual mode for entering and exiting Dawson's bedroom.

"You should stay. We can talk about this."

Joey whirled around. "You can sit in your bedroom forever and write pithy dialogue for us, Dawson, but it's meaning-free. Within these four walls you are utterly safe. No need to take any chances. No need to be bold. But out there, Dawson, is real life. And what I know about real life could fit into a thimble with room to spare. So you just stay in your room, Dawson, if that's what you want. But pardon me if I want to find out what's in that big, bad world besides Dawson Leery." She climbed through the open window.

"Joey, wait!" Dawson called.

But it was too late. She was already gone.

From next door, Jen Lindley saw Joey climb down the ladder from Dawson's room, small clouds of

Joey's breath forming in the cold New England night air.

Jen tried to feel detached. After all, she and Dawson had not been a couple for a long time. She was the one who had broken off their relationship. So there was really no reason for her to feel anything at all about Joey not spending the night with him.

Then why did she feel so relieved?

Because you're insane, she answered herself, as she saw Joey trot toward the edge of the creek—a lagoon, really—where she'd beached the rowboat that would take her home.

Jen turned away from the window and stared at her reflection in the dresser mirror. How could she look so okay on the outside and feel so *not* okay on the inside?

What she felt was lonely. And it was her own fault. After all, she was the one who had broken up with Dawson.

She tried to remember why she'd done it. Ever since she'd been old enough to realize that boys and girls were different, she'd had a boyfriend. But who was she, Jen, on her own? She'd have to fly solo to find out. So, good-bye Dawson. It had seemed to make sense at the time.

Beware of what you ask for and all that. Because now she was on her own, and frankly, it wasn't so terrific.

She'd been so hopeful when she'd left behind her life in New York—parents, friends, and, she hoped, her bad rep—to live with her grandparents in tiny, coastal Capeside. Here she could start fresh. But then her beloved Gramps had had a stroke and died. And Grams was more interested in her own relationship with the Lord than she was in a real relationship with her granddaughter.

The kids at Capeside High hadn't exactly welcomed her with open arms, either. But for a while, there had at least been Dawson. She plopped down on her bed and sighed. "Maybe I should have just stayed in New York."

"Lie down with pigs and you get up dirty," Grams said from the doorway.

Jen looked up. "Excuse me. Were we having a conversation?"

"Your door is open," Grams pointed out. "If you didn't want to be overheard, you should have closed it."

"I'll certainly keep that in mind," Jen replied coldly.

"Jennifer—" Grams began hesitantly, her voice softer.

"Jennifer, what? Please, don't hold back on my account."

Grams sighed. "You don't give me a chance, Jennifer. And that's a pity. You certainly came to Capeside hoping people would give you a chance."

Jen felt a stab of guilt. Her grandmother was right. Sort of.

"I'm sorry," Jen said. "I'm in a weird mood."

Grams nodded tersely. "You might consider praying on it, Jennifer." She disappeared down the hallway.

Jen went to her window again, and looked into Dawson's room. "Petitioning the Lord with prayer doesn't work, Grams," she said, though she was well aware her grandmother was out of earshot. She watched Dawson pull his T-shirt over his head. "If it did, Gramps would still be alive."

Dawson turned out his light.

A lump of loneliness came to her throat. Maybe coming to Capeside really had been a big mistake.

Maybe it was time for her parents to let her come home.

"Pacey?"

Busted!

Pacey Witter froze in the middle of the darkened living room. As his eyes adjusted to the lack of light, he saw his older brother, Doug, sitting on the couch. Doug was a cop. The good son. Which left Pacey only one obvious role to fill.

"Well, if it isn't Deputy Doug," Pacey said, trying for the jocular. "What're you doing, holding a sé-ance for one? Trying to call up the spirit of Rock Hudson?"

"The gay jokes are tired and you know it," Doug said. "It's a school night. Your curfew was two hours ago."

Pacey's anger flared. "Excuse me, I was under the distinct impression I had a father. You're not him."

"I told Dad I'd wait up for you. Why should he lose any more sleep over your antics?" Doug asked.

"Oh, Deputy Doug, your maturity makes me weep!" Pacey sobbed. "I'm not worthy!"

"You're right, you're not."

Pacey sat down next to his brother. "Aw, come on. Lighten up! The thing is, I was with a girl. A great girl. And I lost track of the time. You've been there, right?"

Doug just stared at him.

"Okay, you haven't been there," Pacey allowed. "But you've been with a great guy sometime in your sordid past. Same difference!"

Doug shook his head. "I had this crazy idea you were growing up. But you're the same loser you always were."

The words were like a knife in Pacey's heart. He really thought he should be numb to it by now. It wasn't like he hadn't heard everyone in his family call him a loser every single day of his life.

Doug stood up. "Dad told me to report to him what time you came in. I plan to tell him the truth. There will be repercussions."

"Oh no, Deputy Doug! Not . . . repercussions!" Pacey cried in falsetto.

"Change your life, Pacey," Doug said over his shoulder, as he walked out of the room, "before it's too late."

It was everything Pacey could do not to slam his fist into the wall. At the moment he hated his father, his brother, and the whole stupid, provincial town of Capeside. Even his friendship with Dawson didn't seem like enough reason to hang around.

He banged out of the house, sat on the front porch steps, and fixed his gaze skyward, at the moon.

And all he could think was: Somehow, some way, I've got to get out of this town.

Chapter 2

Jen ran the brush through her hair and checked out her outfit one last time—black boot-cut pants, black cable-knit sweater over a white T-shirt—then grabbed her backpack and headed downstairs. Grams was already in the kitchen, a calico apron over her dress, putting breakfast on the table.

Jen rolled her eyes. As many times as she had told Grams that eating first thing in the morning made her gag, her grandmother still had not gotten the message.

"Toast and oatmeal are on the table," Grams said, going back to the stove to stir something or other.

"Thanks, Grams, but I'm late for school already." Jen poured herself a mug of coffee and sipped it gratefully.

"Sound nutrition is not optional," Grams said.

Jen grabbed a piece of toast. It beat doing the

same old song and dance. She took another long sip of her coffee, then kissed her grandmother's cheek. "Gotta run."

Without turning from the stove, Grams pulled a large, white envelope out of her apron pocket and handed it to Jen.

"What's this?" Jen asked, surprised. The envelope was addressed to her in delicate calligraphy. The return address was in New York City. Clearly it was some kind of invitation. She checked out the postmark.

"Grams, this is two weeks old!" Jen realized.

Her grandmother shrugged. "I just cleared up the pile of bills this morning and there it was. I can't be responsible for keeping track of your things, Jennifer."

"Yeah, right," Jen muttered. "It came from Sin City so you buried it and hoped for the best."

She tore open the envelope. Inside was an embossed invitation to her cousin Courtney's sweet sixteen party, to be held that Saturday night at the Plaza Hotel.

Jen could see Courtney in her mind's eye. Long blond hair, blue eyes, her cousin looked as if she had just stepped out of *Nauseating Female Perfection* magazine. Gorgeous in a completely ordinary way. Honor student. Choir soloist. And the most shallow, self-involved, judgmental witch Jen had ever met.

All Jen's life, she'd been asked why she couldn't be more like Courtney. When Jen pointed out how awful Courtney really was under that perfect exterior of hers, everyone in the family just said Jen was jealous.

"Perfect cousin Courtney is having a perfect sweet sixteen," Jen told Grams.

"Send your regrets in writing, Jennifer. She's very wellbred; it's the wellbred thing to do."

Jen's temper flared. "No point, Grams. Because ill-bred, wicked cousin Jennifer plans to attend." She stuck the invitation in her backpack and headed for the door.

"Jennifer, do you think that's wise?" Gram called.

Jen pushed the door open, then stopped.

"Grams, do you think I care?"

Dawson shoved some of his books into his locker as kids dodged around him, scurrying to class. Joey came up next to him, pointedly ignored him, and spun the combination lock on her own locker.

He had lain awake forever the night before, examining and reexamining, and *re*-reexamining, their relationship. He'd ended up right back where he'd started—wishing that Joey was there next to him. Wishing that *she* wished she was next to him. Like she used to be.

"So, it got cold last night, huh?" Dawson said.

"This is New England, Dawson," Joey said, as she opened her locker and stashed her jacket. "It's supposed to get cold."

"Okay, that was a lame opening line and not the one I had intended to use," Dawson admitted.

Joey shot him a dubious look. Dawson noticed the dark circles under her eyes and a wave of tenderness for her hit him. She lived with her older sister, Bessie, and her sister's baby, Alexander.

Joey's mom had died and her dad was in prison. There was no money. After school, she waitressed at the Ice House. On top of that there was studying, helping with the baby, and cleaning the house.

Compared to Joey's life, Dawson knew he was living in a smiley-faced TV sitcom.

"Did the baby keep you up last night?" Dawson asked, his script for this encounter flying out of his head.

"Just for six hours, the seventh hour I slept beautifully, thanks," Joey said.

"You should have slept at my house. We could have talked about things instead of—"

"This scene is definitely overwritten, Dawson," Joey said. "And I have a splitting headache. So—"

"Joey, Joey, Joey, the woman I adore," Pacey crooned, as he sidled over. He put his hand against her locker and leaned close to her. "You look ravishing today."

Joey shot him a sour look. "What do you want, Pacey?"

"The Marine Bio homework," Pacey admitted.

"Did the concept of studying ever cross your mind?" Dawson asked him.

Pacey put his hands over his heart. "You wound me. How could I study when I was with the bodacious Tia?"

Dawson was surprised. "Tia? As in Tia Swain? Pretty, nice, smart, what-was-she-doing-with-you Tia?"

"That would be her," Pacey agreed. He turned back to Joey. "About that homework—"

"No," Joey said.

13

"Pacey, you actually had a date with Tia Swain?" Dawson asked.

Pacey smiled smugly. "Not only was I with the aforementioned babe, she asked me to take her to the Nightshade concert in Albany on Saturday night."

"Get real," Joey scoffed.

"I am beyond real, Joey," Pacey said. "Picture it. Me. Tia. All alone in Albany for the weekend."

Joey snorted back a laugh. "Right, Pacey. Tia Swain is going away with you for the weekend. What will be your mode of transportation, your bicycle?"

"As the proud possessor of a Massachusetts driver's license—" Pacey began.

"Finally," interrupted Joey.

"—I plan to use a truck, thank you very much," Pacey said, ignoring Joey's comment. "I am formulating final plans even as we speak."

"You're going to take your dad's truck?" Dawson asked. "He'll kill you."

"Details are still pending," Pacey admitted. He turned back to Joey. "Meanwhile, it would behoove me to pass the Marine Bio quiz. Flunking does not further the course of true love."

Joey rolled her eyes.

Pacey clasped his hands together in Joey's face. "Please-please-please," he begged. "I'd get on the floor and grovel but as I recall this is the exact spot where Roger Fulford lost his lunch last week."

"Actually, Pacey, before you interrupted us Joey and I were talking—"

"No," Joey said. *"You* were talking, Dawson."

14

She turned to Pacey. "Walk me to class. I'll talk you through the Cliffs Notes version so you can pass the quiz."

"You are saving my life," Pacey told her.

Dawson watched them walk away. Joey even looked beautiful from the back.

"Hey, Dawson," Jen said, walking up to him.

"Hi." He didn't look at her. Jen's eyes followed his, and she saw that he was zeroed in on the retreating Joey.

Jen leaned against Joey's closed locker. "So, I was thinking of running naked through the halls today. What do you think?"

Dawson tore his eyes from Joey and looked blankly at Jen. "Sorry. Did you say something?"

"Evidently not. Later." She headed for class. So much for Dawson. Clearly he belonged to Joey now. Even if Joey has cut him loose. Relationships were just so insane.

"Hey, Jen," Cliff Elliot said, falling in next to her as she walked down the hall. "You look great today."

With his perfectly chiseled face and tall, hunky body, so did Cliff. But though that thought registered on Jen's brain, no feeling accompanied it.

"Thanks," Jen said. They headed into the bio lab.

"Did I mention that I'm getting into photography?" Cliff asked. "It sort of accompanies my interest in film."

"Uh-huh," Jen replied diffidently, as she chose a seat in the back of the classroom. As far as she had seen, Cliff had absolutely no talent for film, whereas Dawson—

Forget Dawson, she ordered herself.

"I was thinking maybe you could pose for me sometime," Cliff said. He slid into the seat next to her.

"Maybe," Jen said vaguely.

From across the room, Nellie Olson, who Jen suspected was in love with Cliff, shot Jen a wicked look. With her bouncing curls, pink-lipsticked pouty mouth, and evil eyes, Nellie looked like a teen Shirley Temple on acid. She strolled over toward them and slid onto Cliff's desk.

"Well, if it isn't Jessica Rabbit," Nellie cooed nastily to Jen. "Nice outfit. It hides your thighs."

The bell rang shrilly.

"Miss Olson, I believe you have a seat?" Mr. Brinson called drolly from the front of the room. "Let's open our books to page sixty-two, the life cycle of spiders—arachnids."

Jen pulled out her biology book, and the invitation to Courtney's sweet sixteen fell out of it. She picked it up and looked at it. Was she really going, or had she just said that to tick Grams off?

"After the male spider impregnates the female," Mr. Brinson droned from the front of the room, "she no longer has any use for him, so she kills him."

Cliff caught Jen's eye. "Dangerous, huh?"

Jen shrugged.

Nah. Dangerous was going back to New York, even for the weekend. Back to all that temptation. Back to her old boyfriend, Billy.

Back to the scene of her crimes.

* * *

Joey yawned, leaned against the wall of the gym, and watched the girls practicing foul shots on the basketball court under the gung-ho supervision of Miss Gaglia, their estrogen-challenged gym teacher. Baby Alexander had been up all night, screaming from an ear infection, and sleep deprivation was taking its toll. Every time Gaglia blew her whistle, the shriek echoed off the walls and right through Joey's head.

"Let's hustle, ladies! Let's see you guys sink a few!" Miss Gaglia blew her whistle again.

Joey winced. "I'd like to take that whistle and—"

"Me, too," Jen said, as she came out of the girls' locker room in her gym uniform.

Joey looked over at her. Even though she knew it was stupid, she still felt insecure every time she was around Jen. Jen was sophisticated, beautiful, and rich. From day one, she had seen Dawson's IQ slump every time he looked at her. At the time, it had broken Joey's heart.

All that's over now, Joey thought. So why when I look at her do I still feel like I'm Janeane Garofalo and she's Uma Thurman?

Out on the court, Miss Gaglia blew her beloved whistle again. "Not like that, Olson!" Nellie had just taken a pathetic underhanded shot at the basket. "You throw like a girl!"

"*Quelle* surprise," Joey said. "Nellie reeks of girl."

"My guess is, she's overcompensating for a serious case of gender confusion," Jen said.

Joey laughed. "Meaning Nellie was formerly Nelson?"

"Exactly," Jen agreed.

"Not a pretty thought." Joey chuckled again. It was funny. It it hadn't been for all that angst last year with Dawson, maybe she and Jen would have been friends.

Yeah, right. Sexy, sophisticated New Yorker Jen and tomboy, small-town poor girl Joey, buds. Sure.

Gaglia blew her whistle again. "New group, on the court, let's hustle!" She looked pointedly over at Joey and Jen. "In this lifetime, ladies?"

"Next round," Jen called to her.

Miss Gaglia gave Jen and Joey a look of disgust and turned back to the court. Jen and Joey slid down the wall and sat on the wooden gym floor.

"So, how's life?" Jen asked carefully. She had vowed to herself that she wouldn't ask Joey anything about Dawson.

"If you mean 'How's Dawson?,' we're the same non-couple that we were yesterday."

Jen hugged her knees to her chest. "Is that good?"

"I'm too busy enjoying my carefree youth to have a relationship," Joey said blithely. "Haven't you heard? These are the best years of our lives."

"Now, that's a depressing thought," Jen said.

Cliff Elliot and a friend stuck their heads into the gym to check out the girls. As soon as Nellie saw him, she ran to him and threw her arms around his neck.

"Gee, how subtle," Joey remarked. "Maybe Dawson could make a movie about her and call it *Nellie or Nelson?*" Gaglia blew her stupid whistle again, which made Joey wince and rub her temples.

"Headache?" Jen asked, kindly.

"Lately, it's permanent," Joey said. "What I need is a vacation. From everyone and everything."

"Even from Dawson?" Jen asked. She just couldn't seem to help herself.

"Especially from Dawson," Joey replied. "But I might as well dream of winning the lottery, because the odds of my doing either are roughly equivalent."

Miss Gaglia, clearly addicted to the sound of it, blew her whistle yet again and yelled for everyone to hit the locker room. As Jen got up, a thought popped into her mind. About Courtney's sweet sixteen and her own fears about facing everyone in New York.

It wouldn't be so scary if I didn't go by myself, Jen thought. *I could stand to have a human shield. And Joey needs a vacation.*

Jen caught up with Joey in the locker room. "So, is your idea of a vacation big city, or small town?"

"I live in Capeside, USA," Joey said, untying her gym shoes. "What do you think?"

Bingo.

Jen grinned. "Well then, Miss Potter, I'd say you just won the lottery."

Chapter 3

Right after school, Jen headed for the Ice House. She looked around for Joey. The place was jammed—high school kids, stay-at-home moms on outings with their babies, some stray off-season tourists who found Capeside's late autumn chill a quaint experience.

"Hey, Miss, I ordered a veggie burger!" an irate, male voice called from behind her. Jen turned around to see Joey rushing over to the table. Two middle-aged guys with thinning gray ponytails were frowning into their food.

"That is a veggie burger," Joey told the irate guy, trying to keep her own voice calm.

"It looks like turkey," the guy said suspiciously. "I don't eat anything that ever had a face."

"Tofu does not smile, so you're safe," Joey assured him, as she hurried toward the next table.

Jen went to sit at the counter, and ordered a cup of coffee from Bessie, Joey's older sister.

"Joey, your order's up!" Bessie called to her sister.

"Miss, coffee?" a woman asked as Joey hurried by.

"Miss, my check? This is the third time I've asked you."

"Yeah, yeah," Joey hurried behind the counter and began to sling coleslaw into paper cups. "What are you doing here?" she asked Jen.

"Sipping coffee," Jen replied innocently.

"You know what I mean," Joey said. "I already told you I'm not going to New York with you."

It had totally shocked Joey when Jen had invited her. It seemed that Jen wanted to go to her cousin's sweet sixteen at some glitzy hotel in Manhattan, but didn't want to go alone. And Joey was desperate for a big-city vacation. So?

New York! How fantastic would that be? Joey could already picture herself there. Bright lights, big city.

Yeah. Right. Let's just call "Cut!" to that little fantasy, she'd told herself. You are not Audrey Hepburn and this is not *Breakfast at Tiffany's.* You have no clothes for New York. You have no money. You have nothing.

"Reconsider," Jen was saying now, as she stirred a little more Equal into her cup. "You'd really be doing me a favor. The idea of going back there alone doesn't warm my heart."

"And my heart bleeds," Joey said, filling salad bowls.

"Joey, table five says they've been waiting for fif-

21

teen minutes for you to take their order and Tom's not here yet," Bessie said irritably.

"How about if you take it," Joey snapped. "It's *supposed* to be dead in here. I'm *supposed* to be studying."

"Can I help it if everyone in Capeside got hungry this afternoon?" Bessie dropped pickles on the burger plates and loaded them onto a tray, which she handed to Joey. "Go."

"I live to serve," Joey mumbled, hoisting the tray.

Bessie sighed. "Why does she make everything my fault?"

"She needs a vacation," Jen said.

"Yeah, well, don't we all." Bessie hurried to the other end of the counter to take some orders.

Jen turned around and surveyed the noisy restaurant. Two women came in with a group of screaming preschoolers. Bessie had disappeared into the kitchen. Clearly it was more than Joey could handle.

Impetuously, Jen got up, grabbed an order pad from behind the counter, and went over to the table of kids.

"Can I help you?"

"Ten pieces of chocolate cake with chocolate frosting," one of the women ordered, "and ten glasses of milk, please. And two cups of coffee. Black."

"I hate chocolate frosting. Gross! It looks like doody!" one little girl yelled. "I want white frosting!"

"Sorry," Jen said sweetly. "We only have the doody frosting."

Across the restaurant, Joey watched Jen in amazement. They met up as they both put their orders in.

"Thanks for the helping hand, but I'm onto you," Joey said tersely. "You can't guilt-jerk me into going to New York with you."

"Look, I'm not exactly asking you to scrub out toilets with a toothbrush," Jen said irritably. "Some people might look *forward* to a weekend in New York."

"Some people might have the *money* to go, too," Joey shot back. "And the right clothes to wear while they mingle with the rich and ostentatious, but none of those people would be me."

Oh, so *that's* it, Jen thought. I'm an idiot.

"Listen," Jen said, "I'll pay for the train tickets. We'll stay at my parents, so if you don't mind some intentional infliction of emotional distress, that's a freebie, too. And I'll loan you a dress."

"Order up!" Bessie called.

Joey grabbed the food from the warmer and put it on a tray. "Look at this place—it's insane—and this is a weekday. I can't leave Bessie in the lurch for the weekend. So even if I wanted to go, I couldn't."

"Go where?" Bessie asked, overhearing her. She picked up the order slip Jen had taken for the pre-schoolers. "This isn't your handwriting, Joey."

"Jen took it," Joey explained.

"Yeah?" Bessie grinned at Jen. "Cool. So where is it you can't go, Joey?"

"To New York with Jen for the weekend, to some sweet sixteen thing," Joey explained. "I told her it's impossible."

"Go," Bessie said, as she sank the cake knife into

23

a freshly baked chocolate cake with chocolate frosting.

Joey's jaw hung open. "Excuse me? My hearing aid needs adjusting. I thought you just said 'Go.'"

"I did." Bessie deftly slid slices of cake onto plates.

"But what about—" Joey began.

"Read my lips, Joey. Go." Bessie licked chocolate frosting off her pinky. "You need a break."

Joey just stared at her, shocked.

Bessie gently touched Joey's hair. "I know you've cast me as the older sister from hell, but I really do remember what it's like to be a teenager."

"Thanks," Joey said softly. "Really."

"You're welcome, really. Now would you two please get these orders out before the customers mutiny?"

"I was a fool, Derrick. I only pretended not to want you because I was afraid of being hurt again."

"What is it that you do want, Joanne?"

"You. Now. Kiss me. Please, just kiss me."

From behind him, Dawson heard a noise. Joey, climbing through the window. Quickly, he put his computer into "hibernate" mode, blacking out the new dialogue he'd just added to his screenplay. If Joey saw it, she might think it was his fantasy conversation between Dawson and Joey, instead of a scene about Derrick and Joanne.

That would, of course, be a ridiculous assumption.

He was seriously happy to see her. They hadn't

talked since their aborted conversation that morning. Clearly she was avoiding him. But all day at school, after school while he did his homework, and all through dinner with his parents, he'd been thinking about her. Nothing in the world felt right when things weren't right between them. And now, here she was. So clearly, she felt the same way he did.

"Impeccable timing," Dawson said. "I'm starting revisions. I'm thinking of giving Joanne a black belt in karate."

"Derivative," Joey said. "Way too *Buffy*." She closed the window behind her and threw her jacket on his bed. "I didn't row across the frozen lagoon to talk movies."

Dawson smiled. Excellent. She wanted to talk about their relationship. It was about time. He picked up his E.T. doll, and playfully pointed it at her. "Relationship mediator."

"Dawson, your brain is experiencing a meltdown."

He put down E.T. "Fine. No mediation. No movies. Just us. You can go first."

"Big of you, Dawson, but I didn't come over for another fifteen rounds of 'Death By Talking,' either. Actually, I have news."

She told him about her weekend getaway with Jen. New York. The sweet sixteen party at the Plaza Hotel.

He sat on the bed, incredulous. "You and Jen? *Together*? In *New York*? At some rich girl's *sweet sixteen*?"

Joey folded her arms. "I just said that."

"So . . . would a sweet sixteen be a coed sort of an event?"

"No, Dawson," Joey replied evenly. "It's all girls. That is, until the male stripper jumps out of the cake."

"Pardon me if the logic eludes me," Dawson said. "You and Jen have never exactly been soul mates. And I picture Joey Potter at a rich girl's sweet sixteen at the Plaza Hotel about as easily as I picture her eloping with Cliff Elliot."

Joey's eyes blazed with fury. "You're just so sure that hick chick Joey would be the laughingstock of the party, aren't you? Well, it just so happens that—"

"That's not what I meant!" Dawson protested. "I meant that those don't seem like your kind of people."

She sat down next to him. "You've only ever seen me with the so-called human beings of stultifying Capeside. Which, by the by, would include you. So how would you know what my kind of people are?"

Her face was only inches from his. Her hair smelled like a meadow. A movie moment flew into his mind: Joey all dressed up in some sexy dress, dancing in the arms of some oh-so-hip New York type. His name was Stone. No, Brick. He drove a Ferrari. He pulled Joey closer, and—

"Dawson?"

He blinked. The movie moment was gone. Joey remained. Mad. He had hurt her feelings. He hadn't meant to.

"This conversation is not going at all well," Dawson said. "Would you consider take two?"

She nodded. "Consider it considered."

"You just told me you're going to New York with

Jen. My line is: 'While it seems odd that the two of you are going on a trip together, and while as your best friend I have some concerns about your welfare, I hope you have a nice time.' "

"Take two notes: overwritten per usual, but the sentiment was nice," Joey said softly. "Theoretically."

She was sitting so close.

"Theoretically?" Dawson verified

She nodded. "I suggest we go for take three. And Dawson, this time, when you tell me to have a nice time . . ."

"Yes?"

She smiled. "Try to mean it."

Chapter 4

Pacey pounded the basketball down the court, coming to a quick stop at the top of the key. School had let out a half hour ago, and he was killing some time while waiting for Dawson to finish some meeting with Mr. Gold, the film teacher. Then, the two of them would head over to Screenplay, the video store where they both worked.

Pacey head-faked to the left, whirled, and let fly with a jumper. "Yes! And the Celtics go up by a deuce!"

Behind him, someone applauded.

Pacey turned around. Tia Swain, the girl he had been with the night Doug had busted him, stood at the entrance to the gym, smiling. Well, "been with" was a slight exaggeration. Actually, they had run into each other in the library after he had gotten off work at the video store.

But they had talked. That counted. And she *had* mentioned how much she'd like to go to the Nightshade concert in Albany on Saturday, even if that was hours from Capeside. Pacey figured that if she was telling him, then theoretically she'd be willing to go with him. Now all he had to do was connect the dots from the theoretical to the actual.

Tia was a ray of light in the otherwise black doom known as Pacey's history class. Long auburn hair. Green eyes. A smattering of freckles. World's greatest smile.

Which was now aimed at him. Be still my heart.

Pacey sauntered over to her, basketball under his arm. "Please, please, no autographs."

She smiled. "Nice bucket." She cocked her head at him. "Did anyone ever tell you that you look a little like a young George Clooney?"

Clearly the girl was delusional. Cute girls his age *never* flirted with him. But this was definitely a flirting-type conversation. It was beginning to look like the Nightshade concert was not such a long shot after all. All he had to do was "borrow" his father's truck for the weekend. Find some extra money. And then there was the minor detail of actually inviting Tia.

Ease into it, Pacey, he told himself. Don't blow it.

He looked both ways, as if checking to make sure no one was listening. "Actually, I *am* George Clooney."

"Oh, really," she laughed.

Pacey nodded. "Yeah, I'm incognito in this crazy little burg."

29

"Well, I'm just so thrilled to meet you," Tia teased.

Thrilled. The girl had said *thrilled.* Albany was getting closer by the second.

"Actually, pretty lady," Pacey continued in his best George Clooney–type voice, "I'm here doing research for my next project. Very hot. Serious nudity. Wide angle lens. Screen might not be big enough."

"Is this big enough?"

A fist the size of Rhode Island appeared in front of Pacey's face. It belonged to Tom Reynolds, a senior pituitary case who was the starting left defensive end on Capeside's football team.

"Mighty manly meathook you got there, Tom!" Pacey said brightly.

"Who the hell are you, you little twerp?"

"Hey, that would be *Mister* Twerp to you," Pacey said.

Tom got right in Pacey's face. "You think talking dirty to Tia is funny, turd-brain?"

Whoa. Backpedal time. "You've got it all wrong." Pacey feigned astonishment. "Those are lines from a movie!"

A dubious look furrowed Tom's prehistoric-looking brow. At that moment, Dawson came into the gym.

"*His* movie," Pacey said, pointing at Dawson. "Title? *The Big Braggart.* I gotta tell you, the guy's mind is a cesspool."

Tia snorted back a laugh as Tom advanced on Dawson.

"What're you, some kinda sicko freak?" he demanded.

"Missing the beginning makes it so difficult to follow the dramatic thrust," Dawson said, pointedly staring at Pacey.

"Dramatic *thrust?*" Tom grabbed the collar of Dawson's flannel shirt. "That a line from your porno, twerp?"

This time Tia actually laughed out loud. "Come on, Tom," she said, reaching for his hand. "Time to go."

As they walked away, Tom looked over his shoulder and pointed at Dawson. "I've got my eye on you."

"Tom, you're beautiful when you're angry," Pacey called to him.

Dawson stared at Pacey. "Have you lost what little mind you might have at one time possessed?"

Pacey nodded. "Most likely. It seems The Terminator and Tia are an item. But I could swear she was sending me signals."

They left the gym and headed out of the building, taking the side door to assure that they wouldn't run into Big Tom, and cut across the lawn to the bike stand in the parking lot.

"I was *this close* to cinching my date with Tia to the Nightshade concert." Pacey held his thumb and forefinger a fraction of an inch apart. "I mean it. *This close.*"

"Too bad," Dawson sympathized, unlocking his bike.

Pacey sighed. "It's probably for the best. Look at it this way. If we'd gone away together for the weekend, I would have fallen madly in love with her. But eventually, I would have done something monumentally stupid to screw it up, she'd drop me, and my heart would be broken. This way I never have to go through any of that."

"There may be something to your bizarre logic," Dawson admitted, thinking about the sleepless night he'd just spent staring at the ceiling and thinking about Joey.

"Absolutely," Pacey said. "I mean, look at you, going crazy over this weekend in New York thing with Joey and Jen. A loser like me never has to deal with that."

Dawson had told Pacey about Joey and Jen's impending New York road trip during lunch. Pacey thought it was a hoot. He had titled it "The She-Devils Shift Into Overdrive."

They got on their bikes and headed for Screenplay. As they passed the Ice House, they saw Jen and Joey in front, talking and laughing. Dawson couldn't take his eyes off of them.

Honk! Ho-o-onk!

Dawson's eyes darted back to the road, as he barely swerved out of the way of an oncoming car.

"Dying young is highly overrated." Pacey said, as they locked their bikes in front of Screenplay.

"Isn't it strange to see them together?" Dawson asked, as they went inside and got their black Screenplay Video vests from underneath the counter.

"Together without you, you mean." Pacey slipped on his black vest. "Maybe they're bonding over war stories about love-'em-and-leave-'em Leery."

"The painful truth is, I didn't do anything," Dawson reminded Pacey. "They both broke up with me.

Besides, Joey and Jen are both much too evolved to discuss their relationship with me with each other."

Pacey laughed. "Yeah, dream on, my man."

"You're late," Nellie accused, advancing on them, a huge stack of videos in her arms. "My father pays you to be on time. And I hope you two don't think I plan to stock the returns by myself." She placed the videos on the counter, and a couple managed to fall to the floor.

"Never." Pacey bent over to pick up the fallen videos. "That requires alphabetical order. Which implies a working knowledge of the alphabet."

Nellie gave him a withering look. "Multiple choice: Who is practically flunking out of school? A—Nellie. B—Dawson. C—Pacey. Anyone? Bueller? I love no-brainers like that." She flounced back to the comedy section.

"The brain-free always do," Pacey called after her. He turned to Dawson. "I ask you, why isn't Tom Reynolds with Nellie instead of Tia? What could a gorgeous, smart, and did I mention gorgeous girl like Tia see in that mutant?"

"Maybe attraction takes place on some basic biological level over which we have no real control," Dawson mused, as he logged the recent video returns into the computer. "For the species to survive, it makes sense that females are attracted to the males who can best protect them."

The movie moment Dawson did not want to see flashed in his head again. Joey in New York, in the manly arms of some guy with Leonardo DiCaprio's face and Arnold Schwarzenegger's body. Brick Studly. Brick pulled her to him, and—

Cut. He forced the image away and looked at the next video title. *Carnal Knowledge*. Great.

Pacey eyed him and grinned. "I am so onto you, Dawson. You're thinking about Joey. Like what if she meets some genetically superior stud in New York."

"Biology is not destiny," Dawson insisted. He logged in the next film. "Besides, while Joey and I might not be, at this moment, a so-called couple, you underestimate her commitment to our past and future relationship."

Pacey laughed. "Get over yourself! The truth is, you're scared spitless that Joey will find some hunka burnin' love in New York who'll get her to cruise in the fast lane, while you're here in Capeside stuck in neutral."

"You miss the point, Pacey," Dawson insisted. "My concern is the best-friend variety. I'm worried about her."

"For the Jeep and the Tahiti vacation, who is Dawson Leery really worried about?" Pacey asked in his best game-show-host voice. "I'll need that answer, contestant number one—"

"Hey, we're missing a *Liar, Liar* back here!" Nellie called from the video racks.

"Yes!" Pacey yelled, pumping his fist in the air. "Vanna, show the girl with the wet brain what she's won!"

"I heard that," Nellie called. "You'll pay, Pacey."

"Oooh," Pacey called back. "Beat me with your curls."

Dawson leaned against the wall. "The truth, Pacey?"

Pacey grinned. "A delightful change of pace."

"I keep seeing this horror movie moment in my mind," Dawson admitted. "Joey's in New York with this guy, and—"

"Oh, I'm good," Pacey interrupted, as a look of devilish glee spread over his face.

"Does an explanation come with that statement?"

"A plot is forming," Pacey said slowly, "which will close your little horror flick before it opens. The beauty part is that it gets you what you want—Joey. And it gets me what I want—out of Capeside."

"Does logic play any part in this?" Dawson asked.

Pacey made a square with his fingers as if he was framing a shot. "Opening credits. Followed by us, two wild and crazy guys liberating my father's pickup truck after work tomorrow. You tell your parents you're at my house, I say I'm at yours. Next stop, New York. You and Joey. And thank you, yes, I am a god."

"Flawed plot, Pacey. What if my parents call?"

"Flawed characterizations, Dawson. Your parents never check up on you because you are disgustingly trustworthy."

Dawson knew it was a bad idea. Joey was her own person and she made her own decisions. So if she wanted to be with some guy, she had every right to be with him, even if his name was Brick.

Or Buck.

Or Bulge.

Dawson felt sick.

He gave reason one last try. "Your father will miss his truck, Pacey."

"Wrong. Dad and Deputy Doug will be at a Juvenile Justice Convention in Hartford this weekend, plotting a future police state—that's how I knew I could get the truck for my fantasy weekend rendezvous with Tia."

"Which is the only reason you want to do this, Pacey. In your mind, you were already in that truck, on the road with Tia. But that doesn't make this a good idea."

"No, it doesn't," Pacey agreed. "Because this was already a good idea. We'll have the truck back on Sunday. Dad and Deputy Doug will never know it was gone." He hit Dawson in the bicep. "Or would you rather leave Joey in the arms of Studman?"

Dawson's jaw set. "Tomorrow night, we're outta here."

Joey handed her ticket to the conductor, and he handed her back the stub. She could hardly believe she was here, on a train bound for New York, with Jen Lindley of all people, former love of Dawson's life.

At least I hope it's former, popped into her mind.

Whoa. Those were feelings best left unexamined.

She looked over at Jen, who was watching the countryside pass by out the window. Jen had on jeans and an expensive-looking black sweater. Over that she had on a leather jacket that must have cost more than Joey's entire wardrobe.

Joey looked down at her T-shirt, flannel shirt, and denim jacket combo. Swell.

"I can't believe I'm going back," Jen murmured.

"Is that a good 'I can't believe' or a bad 'I can't believe'?" Joey asked.

"Both," Jen admitted. "I miss the excitement. And my friends. But I don't miss the person I was back then. I did some seriously dumb stuff."

"Who hasn't?" Joey asked breezily.

"I had this really wild rep," Jen said slowly. "Some of it I earned. Some of it I didn't. So when I go back—"

"People have long memories," Joey filled in. "Got it."

"And then there are my parents. My father once asked my mother if I got the slut gene from her side of the family."

"Ouch."

Jen turned to her. "I probably should prepare you for the shocking family drama that is about to encompass you in Surround Sound."

"Please. You're talking to Miss Capeside-family-scandal-of-the-decade, here. I walk down the street and people part like the Red Sea."

"Maybe you'll understand, then," Jen said. "My father is . . ." She stopped herself and gave a short, bitter laugh. "I guess that's the problem. I have no earthly idea who my father is. A benevolent despot. Minus benevolence."

"What about your mom?"

Jen shrugged. "Never met a face-lift she didn't like. Majored in MasterCard." She hesitated. "The truth is, I don't know either one of them. And they don't know me."

"Well, I don't exactly know dear old dad, the

felon, either," Joey said. She fiddled with one ear-ring. "It was different with my mom, though."

"You must really miss her," Jen said.

Joey got a faraway look in her eye. "She was one of those people who really listens, you know? Like, when she was with you, she was a hundred percent with you. Even if you were a little kid, she made you feel like what you thought and felt was important."

"That must have been great."

Joey nodded. "My mom was the most loving person I ever knew." She blinked. Her eyes focused again on Jen. "But then she got sick and died. How do you make sense of that?"

"I keep thinking that life should make sense, too," Jen told her gently, "but it never does."

For a long moment, they were quiet.

"S'funny," Joey finally said.

"What?"

"I always think the only thing we have in common is our mutually insane relationship with Dawson, but it isn't true. Both of our families belong in the Dysfunctional Family Hall of Fame. And people love to talk about both of us behind our backs."

Jen laughed. "Sisterhood has occurred over less."

A slight smile curled Joey's lips. "Yeah," she said. "Maybe it has."

Chapter 5

Jen paid the taxi driver while Joey stood on the sidewalk, staring up at Jen's modern high-rise apartment building. A uniformed doorman stood in front of the ornate doors. Through the glass, she could see a huge lobby decorated like some rich person's living room. Large burgundy leather couches. Gleaming mahogany tables. A huge vase of fresh flowers on a marble pedestal. Another uniformed doorman sitting behind a large desk.

So this was how the other half lived.

"Ready?" Jen asked, as the taxi took off.

Joey nodded. As nervous as she felt, she wasn't about to let on to Jen, sisterhood or no sisterhood.

"Good evening, Miss Lindley," the doorman said, opening the door for them. "How nice to see you."

"Hi, Sam," Jen said. "This is my friend, Joey Potter."

39

The doorman nodded his head deferentially. Jen waved to another doorman, and they headed for a bank of elevators.

"What floor do you live on?" Joey asked. Anything to cover her sudden attack of nerves.

Jen stabbed a button that read PH.

"P-H?"

"Penthouse."

"Ah, of course," Joey replied.

Jen used her keys to open the front door of her apartment. Inside, it was shadowy and silent. "Maybe they went out for an early dinner or something," Jen said.

She flipped a light switch, and Joey gasped. The living room was huge. Everything was shades of white—the carpet, the couches, the marble tables. Abstract paintings covered the walls.

"Anyone home?" Jen threw her suitcase on the couch. Jen's voice echoed throughout the place. There was no answer. "That's weird," she said. "They knew we were coming."

"Miss Lindley?"

Jennifer turned around. A very thin, sour-faced woman in her fifties was standing there, ramrod straight.

"Yes?" Jen said politely.

"I'm Mrs. Richardson, your parents' new household manager," she said. "They told me you were expected."

"Ah, yet another new household manager," Jen said. "Don't get too used to the job. There's heavy turnover."

Mrs. Richardson ignored Jen's remark. "Your parents asked that I tell you that they were called away on an unexpected business trip."

"Why, how unexpected," Jen said dryly. "And you would be here because . . . ?"

"Because they asked that I spend the weekend here in case you need assistance."

Jen laughed bitterly. "Right. You're supposed to keep me in my cage. Deter my wild behavior."

Mrs. Richardson was clearly not amused. "Your parents did inform me that you were not to have any male company in the apartment while they are away."

Jen turned to Joey. "Darn. I guess that orgy we had planned is out now, huh?"

"Is there anything you need?" Mrs. Richardson asked.

"World peace?" Jen ventured. Mrs. Richardson didn't crack a smile.

"I'm kidding," Jen told her. "You know. Deflecting a strange situation with humor?"

"I'll be in the manager's quarters if you need me," Mrs. Richardson replied, and walked away.

"It's so heartwarming to see what a priority my parents have made my homecoming," Jen said. She picked up her small suitcase. "Come on."

She led Joey down a hallway to her bedroom and opened the door. Joey was again in awe. Framed posters from rock concerts, some of them signed, lined the walls. The huge platform bed was covered with a velvet tapestry quilt and a dozen ornate velvet and tapestry pillows.

She walked over to take a look at the signed Smashing Pumpkins poster. Next to it was a photo of Jen and another girl with the band. "Friends of yours?"

"My friend's mom books for William Morris Agency," Jen said, as she pulled stuff out of her backpack. "She gets us backstage passes."

Backstage passes, Joey thought. I would kill for backstage passes. She says it like it's so been-there-done-that. Well, for her it probably is. Joey caught a glimpse of her reflection in the mirror over Jen's dresser. She just looked so, so . . . hick. Tall, dark, and hick.

"You can throw your stuff in the closet." Jen cocked her head toward the double closet doors.

Joey opened them and was assaulted by the scent of roses. The closet was as big as her entire bedroom in Capeside. There were already enough clothes in there to stock a small department store. Row after row of gorgeous clothes hung on pristine white quilted hangers.

What the heck am I doing here? Joey asked herself. She dropped her backpack and closed the door. She looked around for Jen. The room was empty.

"Out here!" Jen called.

Joey hadn't noticed the patio balcony off of Jen's room. She walked outside. And there it was—the night skyline of New York City. The skyscrapers glittered like towers of jewels that Joey knew she could never have.

"Wow," Joey breathed, the air cold on her face.

"Yeah," Jen said softly, leaning against the balcony. "I missed this."

"It's so . . . immense," Joey said.

"Not exactly Capeside, huh?" Jen asked with a chuckle.

"What's Capeside?" Joey murmured. Suddenly she got the most incredible, tingly feeling in the pit of her stomach. "It's like everything is possible here. Like you could be anyone. Reinvent yourself."

"Just watch your back," Jen advised. "All that glitters out there is definitely not gold."

"Who's talking gold?" Joey said softly. "Maybe I just want glitter for a while." Suddenly she didn't care if she belonged here or not. She *was* here. So New York could just deal with it.

Jen turned to her. "So, you up for it?"

"For what?"

"Checking out the glitter," Jen said. "You didn't really want to hang out here all night, did you?"

Joey grinned. "Definitely not."

"Tomorrow we can do the tourist stuff if you want—Statue of Liberty, Empire State Building—it's funny, when you live here you never go to those things. But tonight I thought we'd go down to Soho."

"Which is?"

"A neighborhood downtown," Jen explained. "Lots of clubs. Very happening."

"Works for me," Joey said. "Uh . . . what do you wear?"

Jen shrugged. "Whatever."

Joey tried to stifle her impatience. It was easy for Jen to say "whatever." Jen had a closet full of "whatevers" and the sophistication to match. But just as Joey was about to explain this to Jen, Mrs. Richardson knocked on the glass doors to the balcony.

43

"Excuse me, but I called from the hallway a number of times and you didn't hear me," the older woman said.

"What is it?" Jen asked.

"The doorman says a young man by the name of Billy is downstairs for you."

Billy. She had once thought he was the love of her life. Little did she know he was simply the *lust* of her life. At one time she would have done anything for him. She almost did. But moving to Capeside and getting far away from him had probably saved her life. Even if it hadn't been her idea.

Billy had shown up in Capeside once. He'd wanted her back. The person she had become in Capeside had told him to leave. But it was scary. Just being near him had brought back all those old feelings of wanting. And now here he was, waiting downstairs. As if he had read her mind.

Well, she could handle it. Joey was here. Everything was under control.

"You can tell him to come up," Jen said.

Mrs. Richardson hesitated. "Your parents said—"

"Put it in your bad girl report on me," Jen said. "Item one: had guy upstairs within first half hour—something like that."

"I suggest you go downstairs to see your friend," the older woman said.

Jen gave her a look and went into her bedroom, where she pressed a button on an intercom grid in the wall.

"Yes?" came a staticky male voice through the grid.

"Send Billy up," Jen said.

"Very good," the voice said.

Jen turned to Mrs. Richardson. "Look, I'm a big girl, okay? I don't need a baby-sitter."

The older woman walked stiffly out of the room, her body language reeking disapproval.

"Geez, she must take lessons from Grams," Jen said.

Joey watched the woman leave. Jen might not worry about the woman getting fired, because Jen didn't ever have to think about money. But Joey did.

"Will your parents be mad at her?"

"If you mean will they fire her, the answer is probably yes," Jen said. "But firing the help is my mother's main hobby." She went over to her dresser mirror, checked out her reflection, and sprayed some perfume in her hair.

"You want Billy back?" Joey asked. She had met him in Capeside. A serious hunk. Tall. Dark. Very hot.

"No," Jen said.

"Then why the perfume?"

"Simple," Jen said. "I want him to want me."

They went into the living room just as the doorbell rang. Jen took a deep breath and opened it. Billy, leaning against the door frame. He still made her knees weak. The problem was, he made her brain even weaker.

"Hi," he said softly.

"Come on in," Jen said. He did. "You remember Joey? From Capeside?"

"You're friends with that kid Dawson who was hot **for** Jen, right?" Billy asked.

"And you're the guy Jen dumped for that kid Dawson, right?" Joey shot back.

Billy grinned. "You've got a mouth. I like that."

"My thrill level knows no bounds," Joey said dryly.

Jen sat on the back of the sofa. "How did you know I was home, Billy?"

"When it comes to you, Jen, I have radar." He moved closer to her.

She moved away, pretending she needed to straighten the flowers on the coffee table.

Billy looked amused. He knew the effect he had on her. "Besides, word got around that you were coming back for Courtney's sweet sixteen. I figured you'd show up tonight."

Jen moved closer to Joey, as if she was seeking her protection. "So, we were thinking of hitting Soho. Joey's never been."

"That right, Joey?" Billy asked laconically. "Is the small-town girl ready to get wild in the big bad city?"

"Who writes your dialogue?" Joey asked. "It sucks."

Billy laughed. He turned to Jen. "Everyone's going to The Cellar later. They made me promise to get you to come, on pain of death."

"We might cruise by," Jen said casually.

"Good. I'll be waiting." Slowly he walked over to her, and touched her lips with one outstretched finger. Then he turned and sauntered to the door. "Ladies," he said, nodding his head slightly. Then he was gone.

"Is it my imagination, or did he just make your temperature rise and your IQ fall?" Joey asked.

"I hate that," Jen said, plopping down on the couch. She put her head in her hands. "And I hate that I'm so obvious about it. He just . . . he still *gets* to me."

Like Dawson gets to me, Joey thought. No. Forget Dawson. You are over him, so banish him from your mind, she instructed herself.

She sat down next to Jen. "The way I see it, there are lots of guys who can make your hormones dance."

Jen laughed. "Billy makes mine party way too hard."

And Dawson makes mine—Joey stopped herself. No. He *used* to make mine. Past tense. She jumped up from the couch, dragging Jen up, too.

"Listen, what we need here is a lot less brooding and a lot more playing."

Jen cocked her head at Joey. "You know, you're right. My brain is just about brooded out."

"Mine, too," Joey said. "The way I see it, I have forty-eight hours to be Cinderella. Then I turn back into the scullery maid. So I am up for anything."

Jen raised her eyebrows. "Anything?"

"Anything," Joey confirmed. "Let's go be bad."

Chapter 6

"I was thinking of something cheerful," the
skinny, teenaged guy with the bad skin whined.
"What's the most cheerful movie you can think of?"

"*Revenge of the Nerds?*" Pacey suggested.

The guy shook his head. "Too depressing. I used
to be one."

Buddy, I hate to break it to you, Pacey thought,
but it's ten-thirty on Friday night and you're in here
by your lonesome. You still *are* one. He checked
his watch. Only thirty minutes until Screenplay
closed. And then it was bye-bye Capeside, hello
New York.

So far the plan was rolling. Dawson's parents
hadn't blinked when he'd told them he was spending the weekend at Pacey's. And when Pacey had
told his dad, the Chief of Police, that he'd be hanging with Dawson, his father had barely grunted. The

Chief of Police was too jazzed about going to the Juvenile Justice Convention with Deputy Doug, the good son, to pay much attention to the bad seed, Pacey.

Which was exactly how the bad seed had planned it.

"How about an action movie?" Pacey asked.

"Butt Bongo Babes in Toyland?" the nerd smirked.

Pacey spotted Nellie in the action movie aisle. "See that blonde over there? With the curls? She is an expert on action, if you know what I mean." He winked meaningfully.

The guy looked over at Nellie. "Oh yeah?"

Pacey leaned close. "Between you and me, I saw her looking at you before. She wants you. Bad."

The nerd blew into his hand to check his breath, then headed for Nellie, action queen. Dawson rang a woman up at the register. "Due back on Tuesday," he told her.

"I can't wait to get out of here," Pacey said. He checked his watch again. "Twenty-eight minutes and counting."

"I have to tell you, Pacey, I still have some ambivalence about following Joey to New York," Dawson said. "Any good relationship by definition is based on mutual trust."

"Dawson?" Pacey asked.

"Yeah?"

"Stuff a sock in it." Pacey checked his watch again.

From the action aisle, Nellie screamed and

punched the nerd hard in his arm. "You cretin! Get away from me!"

Pacey sighed. "And I had so hoped it was a match made in heaven."

"Hello, Pacey. Dawson."

Abby Morgan, a girl in their class whom neither of them could stand, stood in front of them, a smug grin on her face.

"Abby," Dawson said, nodding. "How's life?"

"Fantastic, Dawson," Abby said. "When I think that it's Friday night and I'm totally free, while you two are slaving away in those dweeby black vests, I get this really happy feeling inside."

"Hey, Ab, your date is waiting for you in the action aisle," Pacey said, cocking his head toward the nerd, who was still hovering around Nellie, giving her lingering looks.

"Nah, he's more your type, Pacey," Abby said. "Actually, I'm here to meet Nellie. We're going to a party. To which neither of you were invited, boo-hoo."

"Not to worry, Ab. Say, is that short for 'abnormal'?" Pacey mused. "Anyway, we've made alternate plans."

"Wow, that's a relief," Abby said sarcastically. "Catch you later, Vest Boys." She sauntered over to Nellie.

"Somehow their friendship does not surprise me," Dawson said. He rang up an older woman renting a stack of exercise videos.

Pacey checked his watch yet again. "Twenty minutes and we are so outta here."

Dawson pulled a sheet of notebook paper out of his back pocket. "Let's review our checklist."

Pacey arched one eyebrow. "We have a checklist?"

"Number one," Dawson read, "pack video camera."

"It's in the truck graciously donated to us, albeit without his knowledge, by dear old dad. While he and Deputy Doug are in Hartford at the Juvenile Justice confab, we'll be using said truck for our great escape. There's a certain poetic justice in that, Dawson."

"Two, gas up truck," Dawson read.

"Done," Pacey said.

"Number three, pack clothes."

Pacey grabbed the list from Dawson. "At this rate we'll still be here Monday morning when it's time to go back to the mind-numbing hell laughingly known as school."

His eyes scanned the list. "Sleeping bags, junk food, stash of great tapes—check, check, and check." He handed the checklist back to Dawson.

"Hey, do either of you guys actually work here?"

They looked up. A pretty girl in a low-cut sweater stood there, holding a video. Neither of them had ever seen her before.

"Hel-lo," Pacey said, pushing in front of Dawson. "I definitely work here. And I'd be thrilled to assist you with anything at all."

"Just the video," the girl said, handing it to him.

Pacey looked at it—*Nightshade: Socrates' Cocktail.* It was a documentary about the band's last tour. Pacey grinned at the girl. "The moment I saw you I knew we had a lot in common. I'm a huge Nightshade fan."

"Really?" She looked amused.

Pacey nodded. "As a matter of fact, me and my bud here are doing a little road trip to Albany for the weekend. Catch their concert, hang with the band, you know." He leaned toward her on the counter. "Maybe you'd like to come along, we could hook you up."

"Sure," the girl said. "I'll just tell my husband. He's waiting in the car." She waggled her left hand in the air, showing him her wedding band.

Pacey straightened up. "On second thought, the truck is a two-seater. Some other time, though." He quickly rang up her rental, and she left.

"Do you consider it your moral duty to hit on anything with breasts?" Dawson asked him.

"Pretty much," Pacey said.

"What would you have done if she had said yes?"

"Sadly, there was very little chance of that," he admitted, checking his watch again. "On a brighter note, that little encounter brought us four minutes closer to the great escape."

Dawson took off his vest and stashed it under the counter. "I still have some concerns, Pacey. Call it what you will, basically you've stolen your father's truck. And we both lied to our parents. If they find out, we are grounded for life."

"Yeah," Pacey agreed. "So what's your point?"

Dawson sighed. Enumerating to Pacey the many things that could go wrong was an obvious waste of time. And dwelling on his guilt over lying to his parents would only make him feel worse.

"No point," Dawson admitted. "I am, for once, point-free."

"There you go," Pacey agreed. He threw his vest under the counter, too. "It's Nellie's turn to close, so we're bustin' outta this burg. I'm telling you, nothing can possibly go wrong."

From behind the foreign film rack, which was taller than she was, Abby smiled.

She had heard everything.

Something certainly can go wrong, she thought, grinning maliciously. And I'm just the girl to make it happen.

Joey looked down at herself and gulped hard. "This is possibly the worst idea in the history of bad ideas."

"Are you kidding?" Jen asked. "You look gorgeous. Look in the mirror!"

Joey did. Staring back was her, but not her. Her long brown hair had been set on large hot rollers. Parted on the side, it fell across her face like a forties movie star's. She, who rarely wore makeup, had on mascara, black eyeliner, and dark red lipstick. Her outfit, on loan from Jen, was all black: a long, skinny, Lycra skirt that began well below her navel, and a matching top that ended well above it.

"I look very bizarre," Joey decided.

"Very tasty, I mean it," Jen said. "I never even wore that skirt because I kept meaning to get it shortened—it puddles around my feet. But it's perfect on you."

Joey sighed. "You have clothes in your closet that

you've never worn, and I have clothes in my closet I've been wearing since I hit puberty."

"Keep the skirt," Jen said carelessly, as she put on some lipstick.

Joey's temper flared. "I don't need handouts from you. If you thought I was hinting—"

"No, no, I didn't," Jen insisted quickly. "I'm sorry if that's how it sounded. Really."

Joey nodded quickly. Get a grip, she told herself. Jen is being incredibly nice to you. She took in Jen's short dress and sexy, thigh-high black suede boots. "You never wear that stuff in Capeside," she noted.

"I want to fit in, not stand out," Jen said. She dropped her lipstick into her little red satin purse with the black Chinese dragon on it. Then she went into her closet and brought out a black motorcycle jacket. She handed it to Joey.

"What's this?"

"It's freezing out and it'll look great with that," Jen said. "Put it on."

She did. Yes. The motorcycle jacket she liked. Joey smiled at her reflection. "Well, I just decided."

"What?" Jen asked.

She tossed her head sexily at her reflection, then batted her eyelashes at Jen. "I'd go for me."

Laughing, the two of them turned out the lights and headed out of the apartment. Instead of going out for dinner, they had ordered in Chinese. Joey decided it was the best food she had ever eaten. Now they finally were on their way to The Cellar to meet Jen's friends. And Billy.

"So, what is this place, The Cellar?" Joey asked, as they got into a cab Jen had hailed. The taxi inched back into the center lane, then zoomed down the street.

"Coffeehouse," Jen said, over the music blaring from the driver's radio. "Excruciatingly hip. Friday is open mike night. You never know who you'll hear."

The driver pulled up in front of a dingy building that didn't look like any coffeehouse Joey had ever seen or imagined. They were in the middle of some warehouse district, it looked like.

"Keep the change," Jen told the driver as they got out.

"Thank you," the cabbie said, and pulled away.

She's paying for everything, Joey thought self-consciously. *And there's not a thing I can do about it.* She shivered in Jen's leather jacket. "You sure this is the place? There isn't even a sign."

Jen pointed to a silver plaque not much larger than a business card embedded in the gray stone of the building. THE CELLAR, it read.

"So, like, if you wear glasses you never find it, right?" Joey asked.

"You're supposed to just know," Jen explained. She started to open the door, then stopped. "I just had a big-time attack of nerves."

Joey comically wrapped her arm around Jen's shoulders, and lowered her voice to a bass level. "Don't worry, little lady. I'll protect you."

Jen laughed. "Right. Now I'm *really* worried!"

Chapter 7

At first, Joey couldn't see at all. But as her eyes adjusted, she saw that they were in a hallway. From the other end, she could hear a band playing, a girl singing.

They went down some steps into the dimly lit club. A band played on a tiny stage. The girl singer wore a bikini with a see-through plastic coat over it, and combat boots.

The place was packed with people, almost all young, sitting at round tables, standing four deep at the bar in the back, or lolling on mismatched couches. In the corner, up high, a huge hammock was strung between two floor-to-ceiling poles that glittered with tiny white Christmas lights. A bunch of people were in the hammock, Joey couldn't see exactly how many. One couple was kissing furiously.

I am *so* not in Capeside, Joey thought.

"Jen! Oh my god, it's Jen!" a girl screamed, jumping out of the hammock and running over to them. She had long red hair and wore hip-hugger jeans that showed off her navel ring. She hugged Jen hard. "I can't believe you're here!"

Jen hugged her back. "I'm here," she said. "This is my friend, Joey. Joey, this is Carson. We go to boarding school together. Well, I mean, we used to."

"Yeah, you got out of it, you lucky wench," Carson said, laughing. "Come on, everyone's back there. They all want to see you."

Carson grabbed Jen's hand and began to drag her through the crowd. "Come on, Joey," Jen called over her shoulder. Joey had no choice but to follow.

Carson led Jen to a crowd of people scrunched together on two couches in a dark corner. Everyone screamed when they saw Jen. Someone pulled her onto the couch, and she fell over her old friends, laughing, while everyone hugged her.

Joey just stood there. What else could she do? She felt out of place and horribly self-conscious, like a little girl playing dress-up who hadn't pulled it off very well.

She looked around. In the corner a gorgeous girl with long, straight hair leaned against the wall. She shook her hair out of her eyes and looked exquisitely bored.

That's the look, Joey decided. She shook her hair off her face, tried to look bored, and leaned one hand oh-so-casually against the nearest table.

It toppled over and crashed to the floor.

She was frozen with embarrassment. Until she realized that the music was so loud, and the place was so wild, that no one had even noticed.

A skinny guy wearing a black T-shirt that read THE CELLAR quickly righted the table. "Drink?" he asked her. "There's a minimum. Two."

Drink. This was a coffeehouse, but did the waiter mean alcohol when he said two-drink minimum? She didn't drink. Plus she had no idea how much a drink cost, and had all of twenty-five dollars in her purse. Ten of those dollars had been a gift from Bessie before she left Capeside.

"Uh . . . juice?" Joey asked tentatively.

"We have sixteen kinds of juice and thirty-two kinds of coffee," the guy said impatiently, "and I don't have all night."

"Orange?"

"Racy," the waiter said sarcastically before he took off for the bar.

Okay, so far so terrible, Joey thought. Jen was still in the midst of her friends, laughing and talking, so Joey looked around some more, her eyes sweeping the room. And there he was. The most gorgeous guy, looking straight at her. Tall. Dark hair. Absolutely perfect-looking.

Joey looked away and pretended to be watching the girl singer. When she glanced oh-so-casually in his direction again, the gorgeous guy was gone.

"Hey, Joey!" Jen called to her. Joey moved closer to Jen. "I want you to meet my friends. You guys, this is Joey Potter, a friend of mine from Capeside."

"Hi," Joey said.

Pointing at each of her friends in turn, Jen quickly rattled off their names. Joey tried to keep them straight—Carson with the red hair and the navel ring she had already met. Amy was a preppie type with dark curls. A huge crew-cut guy named Scott had his arm around her. Alexis looked like a model. She had a small tattoo just below her collarbone that Joey couldn't read. Her twin brother Tucker had a sweet face and puppy dog eyes.

"You will be tested on this later," Tucker told Joey from his seat on the couch.

Amy lit a cigarette. "You're so lucky, Joey. I'd love to get my butt out of the city." She exhaled a smoke ring.

"And live without Chinese food delivery?" Joey asked.

"I am so totally sick of Chinese," Alexis said. "I swear, it makes me hurl."

"Yeah, like you don't make yourself hurl, Alex," Carson said, laughing. "Two hurls a day keeps the poundage away."

"That's just a nasty rumor based on the truth," Alexis said airily. "So, what's Capetown like?"

"Cape*side*," Tucker corrected her. "Cape Town would be in South Africa."

"Whatever," Alexis said, annoyed. She turned back to Joey. "So, what's it like?"

"Quiet," Joey said. "Very quiet."

Up on stage, the band finished their number. A few people applauded. A fat guy with a ponytail came out to adjust the equipment for the next act.

"So, I thought Billy was going to be here," Jen said, trying to sound nonchalant.

"He is here," came a low, sexy voice from behind her.

59

Jen turned around.

Billy.

"I was in that crush at the bar," Billy said. "You look fantastic, Jen."

"Thanks." She looked up at him, and got that same old feeling. All the way down to her toes. Then she glanced over at Joey, who shrugged at her.

"Man, it's good to see you," Billy murmured. "Hey, you want a drink?"

"This is a coffeehouse with a juice bar," Jen said. "No alcohol."

Billy laughed. "Get real, Jen. We brought our own." He took an old-fashioned metal flask out of the pocket of his leather jacket. "Strictly high test."

"No thanks," Jen said lightly.

"Oh, come on," Billy said. "Where's my party girl?"

"*Ex*-party girl," Jen reminded him.

Amy laughed and took another hard drag on her cigarette. "Yeah, right, Jen. And I gave up smoking."

"Hey, cut the girl some slack," Billy said, putting his arm around Jen. He threw back a long hit from the flask and then put it in his pocket. "Come sit with me."

Jen looked over at Joey, a question in her eyes. Joey nodded that she was okay, so Jen's friends made room for her and Billy on the couch, while Joey continued to lean against the back of it, doing her best to look cool. The hair that dipped over one eye kept migrating to her mouth each time she moved, where it got stuck in her goopy red lipstick.

She pulled a strand of hair off her lips and looked around again for the beautiful guy she had seen earlier. Gone. A figment of my overheated imagination, Joey thought.

"Would you like a drink?" Tucker asked, craning his neck around from where he sat.

"I already ordered one, thanks."

"In this place, that's meaningless," Tucker said. "I'll go to the bar and get you one, if you want. The fresh papaya-peach juice is great."

No alcohol, he's paying. Perfect, Joey thought. "That would be nice. Thanks."

Tucker got up from the couch and stood eye to eye with her. Or rather, eye to shoulder. He was a good four inches shorter than she was.

Joey smiled down at him and bent her knees a little. If he noticed, he didn't say anything. "Be right back," he promised, and headed for the bar.

The fat guy on stage tapped the microphone. "Okay, our next singer is from Harlem, please welcome the blues styles of Shanda DeWayne."

A couple of people clapped, most people paid no attention. A beautiful black girl in a short white dress took the mike. She began to croon an old blues song into the mike.

"Dance?"

Joey turned around. Standing there, as if she had conjured him up from her dreams, was him.

The perfect guy from across the room.

And he was smiling right into her eyes.

Chapter 8

"Dance where?" Joey asked, looking around. There was no dance floor.

"Anywhere," the guy said. "I'm Danny Fields." He held out his hand.

Joey shook it. "Joey Potter."

Up close, he was even more fantastic-looking then he had seemed from far away. Taller than her. Broad shoulders. A cleft in his chin. One pierced ear. His eyes were electric blue.

"Trust Danny to zero in on the hot new girl," Alexis said, stumbling up from the couch. Apparently she had been drinking. A lot. "Do you have radar or something, Fields?"

"I have eyes," he replied, keeping his glued to Joey.

Alexis leaned in between them drunkenly. "He's got moves, too, Joey," Alexis slurred. "Consider yourself warned. I have to pee so bad." She staggered toward the ladies' room.

Danny didn't take his eyes from Joey's face. It was as if she was the only girl in the universe. "What is Joey short for?"

She refused to say Josephine. *No one* was named Josephine. "Joelle," Joey invented, trying to flip her hair off her face with a casual gesture. It got stuck in her lipstick again, she pulled it free. "My mother is French."

"Beautiful name for a beautiful girl." He released her hand, but smiled into her eyes. "Really. You are really beautiful. You walked in with Jen and I couldn't take my eyes off of you."

Joey was thrilled, but she refused to let it show. She tossed her hair again. "Why do I have the feeling you've said that before?"

He smiled. "Okay, I have. The difference is, this time I mean it."

"And you've said that before, too," Joey said.

This time he didn't smile. "No. I haven't."

He was so hot. Like, movie-star hot. And there he was, flirting with her, tall tomboy Josephine Potter from Capeside, Massachusetts.

Easy, Joey, she told herself. You are not the kind of girl who falls for a guy just because he's hot.

I don't think.

Suddenly, Tucker was there. "Here you go," he said, handing her a frosted glass of juice. "Sorry it took so long, but it's a zoo at the bar."

"Thanks," Joey said. "Uh, do you two know each other?"

Tucker looked up at Danny and nodded tersely.

63

Danny was six inches taller than he was. "I've seen you around. You're a senior, right?"

"Right," Danny agreed. "Hey, thanks for getting my lady a drink." He put his arm around Joey and began to lead her away.

"Oh, sorry," Tucker said quickly, "I didn't realize you two were together."

"We're—" Joey began.

"Catch you later, my man," Danny said.

Joey just looked at him. "We're not together."

He smiled at her. "We're not?"

She looked over her shoulder, back at Tucker. He had already joined his friends again. "It's just that he bought me the drink . . ."

"Those deb manners," Danny said, shaking his head ruefully. "Finishing school finishes you girls off, I mean it. Listen, just because he bought you a glass of juice does not obligate you. Unless you want to be with him instead of me."

He looked into her eyes, and Joey felt as if an electric current was running between them. "No," she said faintly.

"So you want to tell me about yourself? Or would you rather be mysterious?" Danny asked her.

What would you like to know, Joey thought. About my latest fun trip to visit Dad in prison? Or how about the time I sewed some old ribbons around the hem of my jeans when I outgrew them, because I couldn't afford new ones?

I think not.

On the other hand, the time she'd tried to lie about her life to a rich guy she'd met who was on vacation in Capeside, she'd blown it completely. Better to be mysterious and keep her mouth shut.

"There's not much to tell," Joey said breezily. "I'm planning to be either a Victoria's Secret model or a brain surgeon."

Danny laughed. "I love a girl with big dreams."

"I don't want to talk about me," Joey said. I live with me on a daily basis, she added in her mind. And basically, I'm sick of me. "Tell me about you." She took a sip of her juice.

He folded his arms. "Let's see. I'm going to Duke next year—that is if I get in. I'll probably end up in my dad's brokerage firm. And next summer I'm going to bum around Europe with my friends."

Gee, I'll be waitressing at the Ice House, Joey thought. We have so much in common.

A bored-looking girl with two nose rings, carrying a basket overflowing with roses, wandered through the crowd. "Roses. Two dollars. Roses."

"How much for the whole basket?" Danny asked her.

"Got me," the girl said. "I'm not counting 'em all, either."

Danny took a hundred-dollar bill out of his billfold and handed it to her. It was the first hundred-dollar bill Joey had ever seen, outside of the Ice House.

"Cool," the flower girl said, and handed him the basket before she wandered away.

Joey searched her mind for something flip to say. "I think that is what is commonly known as conspicuous consumption."

"I know all about you old-money girls," Danny

said, putting the basket of roses on the nearest table. "You never even carry it with you. You think cash is tacky, right?"

"Right," Joey agreed. She had no idea in the world what he was talking about, except that he seemed to think she was rich—which was kind of hilarious.

Danny took one rose from the basket and broke the flower off the stem. Then he gently put the rose behind Joey's ear.

"Why did you do that?"

"Because, Joelle, you look like a girl who smells like roses." His arms slid around her waist. "And one other reason."

She stared up at him. "What's that?"

"So when I kiss you, I can find out if I was right."

The cold late autumn rain beat down on Pacey's truck like a barrage of shots from a BB gun. He had pulled off the road and into this truck stop an hour ago, when it had started pouring so hard that he couldn't see the highway. And it was still pouring.

"Are we having fun yet?" Dawson asked glumly.

"It has to stop raining soon," Pacey said. He reached into the bag of chips. Nothing left but crumbs.

"We could go into the truck stop and mingle with the outlaws," Pacey suggested. "Pick us up some chewing tobacco or something. Curse, cheat, and lie."

Dawson shot him a look. "We're still in Massachusetts, Pacey. This isn't *Deliverance*."

"Oh, lighten up, Dawson. Look on the bright

side. The rain will stop eventually—I watch the Weather Channel so I know these things—and we are not in Capeside."

"No, we're in a truck stop, in a stolen truck."

"Borrowed," Pacey corrected. "From my father. Which does not exactly warrant a manhunt for the one-armed man, okay?"

For a while they just sat there, listening to the rain. Pacey pushed a Counting Crows tape into the tape deck.

"What do you think Joey's doing right now?" Dawson asked over the music.

Pacey closed his eyes and put his hands on his forehead. "Let Pacey's Psychic Network divine it for you. I see . . . yes! I see Joey with—can it be?— four, no five guys. All of them tall, exceedingly buff specimens. Manly men. One is named Brick. One is named—"

"Your attempt at levity is not appreciated."

Pacey opened his eyes. "Relax, Dawson. It's late. Obviously Joey and Jen are at Jen's apartment."

"With Brick?" Dawson asked.

Pacey shook his head. "Earth to Dawson. You made Brick up. He is a figment of your heated little mind. There is no Brick."

"So Joey is solo."

"At the moment, Han Solo," Pacey agreed.

Dawson drummed his fingers on the dashboard. "It's not that I begrudge her spreading her wings, Pacey. Contrary to her wounding comments to me, I realize there is life outside of my room. I understand that Joey wants the opportunity to experience it. It's just that—"

"You don't want her to experience it with a guy," Pacey put in, "unless the guy is you."

"Joey is much more fragile than she looks or seems," Dawson said. "Her toughness is an act. Even if we aren't romantically involved right now, that doesn't mean my concern for her welfare is any less genuine."

Pacey rolled his eyes. "She's alone, Dawson. In bed. Asleep. Alone."

"You're positive?"

"Positive," Pacey said. "Joey might annoy the hell out of me, but this I know about her. She would not get it on with some guy she just met. I'm telling you, Dawson, you have totally, absolutely nothing to worry about."

Chapter 9

Joey knew that Danny was going to kiss her.

She felt flustered, flushed, dizzy. She took a step away from him. "Who says I want to be kissed?"

He didn't answer her, just took her hand, and led her through the crowd, up the steps, into the long, dark entranceway. From outside she heard a rumble of thunder.

Their eyes locked in the dim light. Another rumble of thunder. The singer's sultry voice wafted over them.

"When he's near me, my brain catches fire.
And I can't hide my desire . . ."

Danny held out his hands. "May I have this dance?"

This is not a dream, Joey, she told herself. This is not a movie. It's real life. Your life.

She stepped into his arms.

Usually she felt self-conscious dancing. But this time, everything fit. They swayed to the music.

"I knew it," he murmured into her hair.

"What, that I'd smell like a hundred-dollar rose?"

"That you'd feel like a million-dollar rose, Joelle."

Joey closed her eyes and gave herself up to the moment. She wanted to feel, not think about the minutia of her sad little life. The scrambling for money. The whispers behind her back about her messed-up family. And the biggest fear of all— that somehow she'd get stuck in Capeside and her life would end up a big, empty nothing.

She didn't want to think about Dawson.

She *especially* didn't want to think about Dawson.

The song ended. Danny stopped moving. He reached for the rose in her hair and pulled off a petal. He ran the petal over her face.

He's going to kiss me, she thought. I'm going to let him. I want him to. Outside she could hear the rain begin.

"Joelle." Danny brought his mouth down to hers.

"Stay the hell away from me, Barry!" a girl screamed, as she ran out of the club, careening against the walls in the hallway. "I hate your guts!"

Joey and Danny broke apart. "You okay?" Joey called to the running girl.

The girl whirled around, breathing hard. Tracks of mascara-blackened tears ran down her cheeks. "Keep him away from me!"

A skinny guy with long black hair stood behind

them. "Get back here, Audrey. I mean it. I'll kick your butt!"

He started after her. Danny stepped in his way. "Hey, chill out, okay?" Danny put his hand on the skinny guy's chest.

"Get outta my face, man!" the skinny guy yelled, pushing Danny's chest. It got him nowhere. "I'll kill you, Audrey! You're dead!" He stabbed the air in her direction.

"You're wasted, Barry," the girl yelled. "I hate you when you get like this!"

Barry tried to get around Danny again, but Danny stopped him. "Why don't you go back in there and get some coffee? Leave the girl alone."

The guy reeled backward drunkenly. "Who the hell are you, butthole, the morals squad?"

"Sure," Danny said. He spun the guy around. "Head back in there and get yourself together, man."

The guy swore under his breath and staggered away.

"Thanks," the girl said. "He only gets like that when he's toasted. Otherwise he's great. Really. We're engaged." She wandered out the door and into the rain.

Joey was not into the macho thing, but she couldn't help but be impressed with how Danny had handled things.

"There is nothing lower than a guy hurting a girl," Danny said, shaking his head.

Joey leaned against the wall. "How about a girl hurting a guy?"

77

"Don't you ever listen to Alice Cooper?" Danny asked. " 'Only women bleed.' "

Joey feigned shock. "Future stockbroker listens to Alice Cooper? How retro!"

Inside the club, a guy began a poetry rant into the mike, something about two-faced girls and broken hearts.

Danny fingered the rose in Joey's hair. "Are you one of those two-faced girls?"

"Yep," Joey said.

He moved even closer. "So in other words, you could be trouble."

"Big time," Joey whispered.

His arms slid around her slender waist. He kissed her. Slowly, sweetly, his lips gently exploring hers. The kiss turned passionate. Her arms went around his neck. Everything fell away—the dark hallway, the poetry rave, the entire world—as Joey kissed him back.

Whoa. The world was spinning. Thunder and lightning. But how could it be, when she didn't even know him?

Stop thinking, she ordered herself. Just feel.

"Joey? Joey!"

She broke away from Danny. Jen was standing in the doorway of the club. Joey smiled at her. Danny's arm was still around her waist.

"Having fun?" Jen said pointedly.

Danny turned to Joey. "Having fun, Joelle?"

"Joelle?" Jen mouthed.

"What Joey is short for," Joey explained quickly.

Jen went along. "Right. I just always forget because no one calls you that."

Danny smiled and pulled Joey close. "I call her that."

"Hey, *Joelle*," Jen said, "come to the ladies' room with me?"

"Why do girls do that?" Danny asked.

Jen grabbed Joey's hand. "We're like wolves, we go in packs."

"I'll be back," Joey told him over her shoulder.

They wormed their way through the crowd to the ladies' room. The walls were covered with graffiti, but it was deliberate—Magic Markers on ropes hung from the walls so people could add their own missives.

There were girls everywhere. One sat crying in the corner while her friend tried to comfort her. Two other girls lolled against the wall, sharing a cigarette. There were six more girls in front of the mirrors, primping.

"Maybe you're not pregnant," a girl with a buzz-cut and a pierced eyebrow said to her friend, as she added blush to her cheeks. "Take the stupid test."

The two girls sharing the cigarette stubbed it out and lit a joint. Joey was shocked, but pretended not to be.

Jen turned to Joey. "So?"

"What?" Joey asked.

"Danny."

"I like him." Joey pulled out her hairbrush and began to brush her Veronica Lake hairdo.

Jen leaned against the wall and watched her. It had been weird seeing Joey with someone besides Dawson. Weird in a good way, Jen had to admit. Maybe Dawson and Joey really were over. The thought did not make her unhappy. Which was also weird, because she didn't want Dawson back. True, she still had feelings for him. But a return to coupledom was not on the horizon. Regardless, she did feel some responsibility to tell Joey the truth about Danny.

"Listen, about Danny Fields," Jen said slowly. "He's a player."

"So?" Joey asked.

"I'm serious. I heard he keeps this chart of every girl he's slept with. He grades them on looks, bod, performance—"

"How do you know it's true?" Joey interrupted.

Jen gave her a look. "Come on, Joey!"

"Let me refresh your memory," Joey said. "People said all kinds of things about you that weren't true. People say all kinds of stuff about *me* that isn't true!"

"It's not the same," Jen insisted. "Look, I'm not trying to tell you what to do, but—"

"Good, don't." Joey touched Jen's hand. "I got it, okay? This is not *Romeo and Juliet.*"

"No, it's *Romeo and Joelle,*" Jen said.

Joey put her brush back in her purse. "I'm having fun. That's all." She disappeared into a stall.

Jen picked up a Magic Marker and began to doodle mindlessly on the wall. I tried to warn her, she thought. She's a big girl. She can make her own decisions.

Joey came out of the stall and washed her hands. "So, how's it going with Billy?"

"Like a moth to a flame, unfortunately."

"You guys getting back together?"

"Maybe," Jen admitted.

They headed back into the club. Jen crossed the room to Billy. He put his arms around her. She smiled up at him. He kissed her.

You can fool yourself, Jen, Joey thought, but you can't fool me. You're not going back to Billy. Because your heart belongs to someone else.

She knew this was true because she had seen what Jen had doodled on the bathroom wall without even realizing she had done it.

A heart. And inside the heart, two initials: J + D. Which is fine, Joey told herself. I'm perfectly okay with it. Dawson and I are much better off as best friends.

So why does the thought of him getting back together with Jen tick me off so much? If I don't want him that way, then why is it that—

"Hey."

Danny. Smiling down at her. Reaching for her hand.

J + D.

"Hey back," she said.

"I missed you, Joelle."

J + D.

A memory of Jen and Dawson, kissing passionately, flew into Joey's mind. She remembered how much it had hurt her, when she wanted Dawson so desperately she thought she'd die if she didn't have him. But he was with Jen.

Now, everything was different. Except the hurt of it was still there. And that was the part of her that didn't want Jen and Dawson to—

"Joelle?"

Joey blinked. "What?"

He touched her cheek. "You were a million miles away."

Just a few hundred. In Capeside.

"I'm right here," Joey said.

"Listen, I know a fantastic after-hours club," Danny said. "They open at midnight. It's private— they don't check ID."

J + D.

Admit it, Joey, she told herself. You don't want Dawson but you don't want Jen to have him, either. You are a small-minded person. You need to do something to get your mind off of them completely. Something radical.

"So, you up for it?" Danny asked. "You'll like the club. It's cozy. Very private."

Something radical. And Danny was so hot. So nice. So . . . hot. Joey reached up and wrapped her arms around Danny's neck. "I have a better idea."

His arms went around her waist. "What's that?"

"Come back to Jen's with me."

Danny's face lit up with pleasure. "Yeah?"

"Yeah," Joey said. "Absolutely."

Chapter 10

"You did *what?*" Jen asked Joey.

"I invited him back to your apartment," Joey said. "What's the problem?"

"Invited who back to Jen's apartment?" Billy asked, coming up next to Jen. He was sipping from a glass of fresh-squeezed juice from the juice bar. Jen knew he'd laced it heavily with vodka.

"Danny," Joey said. She cocked her head toward the other side of the club. "He just went to tell his friends."

"Great," Billy said, slipping an arm around Jen's shoulders. "I'll go tell my friends adios, and the four of us can go party."

"Hold it," Jen said. "Do I have any say in this?"

Billy grinned at her. "You have all the say in the world. Your lips already told me."

Jen made a face. "That is so . . . ick."

Billy laughed. "I'm kidding." He stroked her hair. "But really, Jen. We need to be alone. We have a lot to talk about."

Danny joined them. "All set." He put his arm around Joey. "It's pouring out, and it's hell getting a taxi around here late at night. I called a limo service."

Limo as in limousine, Joey thought. Those long, fancy cars you see stars getting out of at movie premieres. It is *so* not Capeside.

"I love limos," Joey said, smiling at him.

"Good." Danny ran one finger down her forehead, down her nose, until it landed on her lips. "I want us to do everything that you love."

Red alert, Jen thought. Big red alert.

She grabbed Joey's hand. "Uh, I just realized that I need to . . . go back to the ladies' room."

"We were just there," Joey protested.

"Well, we need to go there again." Jen half-dragged Joey through the crowd.

"Why do I feel like I'm starring in a remake of *Groundhog Day*?" Joey asked, when they got back into the ladies' room.

"Look, Joey, those guys are not coming back to my apartment with us."

"Why not?" Joey leaned against the wall. She knew exactly what it said on the wall, just about at the level where her butt met the wood. J + D.

"Because Danny thinks you're inviting him back to have sex with him," Jen said bluntly.

"He does not."

Jen gave her a jaded look.

"Okay, maybe he does," Joey allowed. "That doesn't mean I have to do it."

"Why put yourself in that position?" Jen asked.

"Because I want to kiss him," Joey admitted. "A lot. And I don't see why I can't kiss him—a lot—and then tell him I don't want to go any further."

Jen shook her head. "You don't know him."

"Neither do you," Joey shot back. "Don't you want to be with Billy? You've been doing the vertical bop with him all night. All you lack is the bed and the horizontal."

Jen sighed. "Look, I didn't come here this weekend to get it on with Billy. When I'm with him, something happens to me. It's like, this is my brain—" she gave an intelligent nod, "—and this is my brain on Billy." She let her tongue loll out of her mouth and crossed her eyes.

Joey laughed. "Attractive illustration."

"I just . . . I need some time to think. And I can't think if those guys come home with us. Not to mention the fact that the ever-vigilant Mrs. Richardson will put it in my report card to my parents."

The door banged open and two drunk girls staggered into the bathroom, retching. "Interesting. Getting wasted is just as obnoxious in New York as it is in Capeside," Joey said, making a face. "Let's go."

They went back into the club. On the stage a longhaired guy wailed something unintelligible into the mike.

"Can you just tell Danny the plans have changed?" Jen asked. "And I'll take care of Billy?"

Joey knew that Jen was right. It was stupid to invite Danny and Billy back to the apartment.

Danny would obviously get the wrong idea. As for Billy, just because Joey wanted it to be J + B and not J + D didn't mean she could make it so.

"Okay," Joey relented.

They found the guys in the entranceway to the club.

"Limo's here," Danny told them. "You ready?"

"I need to talk to Billy," Jen said, taking him aside.

Danny turned to Joey, slipped his arms around her waist and nuzzled her hair. "I can't wait to be alone with you."

Joey stepped out of his embrace. This was not going to be easy. "Listen, I kind of . . . I made a mistake."

"I don't understand."

She fiddled with an earring. "I mean that when I invited you back to Jen's, you got the wrong impression."

Danny looked confused. "I did?"

Joey nodded. "You thought I meant I want to . . ."

He grinned. "Because you *do* want to."

"Look, it was an impetuous offer that I didn't really think through," Joey explained.

"I have a feeling that you're one of those girls who does way too much thinking, Joelle."

Right on the first guess. Maybe they were soul mates. And he was *so* hot. She took his hand. "It's not that I don't want to be with you . . ."

He took his hand back. "So then what's the problem?" There was a new, impatient edge to his voice.

"I'm not ready for what you're ready for."

He gave her a cool look. "You don't want it?"

"No."

"Yeah, right," he laughed sardonically. "Girls like you kill me. You want it. You just don't want to take *responsibility* for wanting it."

Suddenly Joey could not figure out what she was doing with him. It was so bizarre. In one split second everything changed. He was cute, but so what? Guppies were cute, too. But they ate their babies.

"Well, it's been swell deluding myself into thinking that you were someone I might want to know," Joey said, backing away from him. "I'll just be going now."

Danny's jaw fell open. "You're not serious."

"It appears that I am," Joey said.

"I don't believe this!" Danny kicked the wall.

"Believe it." Jen said, joining Joey. "You ready?"

Joey nodded. She noticed that Billy was sipping from his drink, eyeing Jen, cool as ever. "There's still tomorrow night," he reminded her.

"Let's go," Jen said, pulling Joey toward the door.

Danny walked over to Billy. "What's up with them, man?"

"Down, big guy," Billy told him. "You'll live."

Jen looked back and smiled at Billy.

Joey zipped up her leather jacket and eyed the downpour outside. "I wish I had an umbrella."

"Hey, Joelle!" Danny called.

Joey turned around.

"The virgin tease act is real tired, you know?" Danny called nastily.

"Excuse me while I go drive my knee through his gonads," Joey told Jen.

Jen stopped her. "I've got a better idea. Come

on." She dashed out into the freezing rain and jumped into the waiting stretch black limo before the driver could even get out of the car. Joey jumped in next to her.

The short, balding driver turned back to them. "You're the Fields party?"

"That would be us," Jen agreed.

The driver pulled away from the curb.

"The dispatcher said to put this on your father's tab, like usual. Going to the home address?" The driver looked in the rearview mirror at them.

"Change of plans," Jen said. She gave him her address.

"You got it," the driver said. "Help yourself to anything in the fridge back there. Classical music okay?"

"Fine," Jen said.

Mozart wafted through the car.

"We stole Danny's limo," Joey mouthed to Jen.

Jen nodded. "He deserved it."

"You were right about him," Joey admitted. She leaned back against the cool leather. "Why is it that if a guy wants a girl just because she's hot, he's a player, but if a girl wants a guy just because he's hot, she's a slut?"

"Labels created by small people with small minds who have a need to put everyone into little boxes because it feels safer," Jen said. "Want to know my fantasy?"

"Does it involve massage oil and see-through lingerie?"

Jen shook her head no. "My fantasy is to be able

to be best friends with a cute guy. No sex, even though he's hot. Just friends."

"Why?" Joey asked.

"Because sex changes everything," Jen said simply. She reached into the fridge and took out a small bottle of sparkling cider. Then she got two champagne glasses from the small, recessed area under the bar, handed one to Joey, and filled them both with cider. "Here's to . . . what?"

"Friendship?" Joey queried.

"Friendship," Jen said. "Like you had with Dawson."

"*Have*," Joey corrected.

"*Had*. You can't go back to where you were before, Joey. What happened in between is always going to color where you are with him now."

"I guess that means it's always going to color where you are with him now, too," Joey said.

Jen gave her a rueful smile. "Yeah," she admitted. "Let's drink to that."

Chapter 11

Dawson woke up shivering inside his mummy-style sleeping bag. Even though he'd zipped it shut before he'd fallen asleep, it hadn't kept the cold out. Now he saw why—there was a huge rip near his left ear. That is, assuming he still *had* a left ear. It was too numb from the cold to tell.

Rubbing his ear back to life, he stuck his head out of the bag like a turtle, and squinted, bleary eyed, into the early morning light. Next to him in the back of the truck, Pacey was still out, snoring loudly. They were parked in a deserted McDonald's parking lot, somewhere in, of all places, Staten Island.

Dawson burrowed down into his sleeping bag again as he recalled just how they had ended up there. Once the rain had slowed down the night before, Pacey had headed for Manhattan. Without a map. Which was no problem, Pacey insisted. He knew exactly where he was going.

Right. They drove in circles—bridges leading to highways leading to tunnels leading to new highways, all of them requiring the payment of tolls, until neither of them had a clue where they were. Dawson finally convinced Pacey to stop and ask for directions, but the only place they found open was a biker bar with a fight in progress in the parking lot. It seemed like a good idea to move on.

They'd traveled on for another half hour when Pacey pointed to the large green sign that led to Manhattan. Ha! Hadn't he said he knew what he was doing? He crossed a bridge, got on something called the FDR Drive, went through something called the Battery Tunnel, all the while bragging about his excellent skills at a navigator.

Then Dawson saw a new sign. A sign that did not fill his heart with joy. Somehow they had crossed the Verrazano Narrows Bridge, which put them on the delightful island borough of—tada!—Staten Island.

Dawson had considered killing Pacey and had only refrained because he didn't know how to drive the truck. It was past four o'clock in the morning and both of them were wiped out. So they'd simply pulled into the parking lot of this McDonald's, and, under the benevolent gaze of a giant plastic Ronald, they'd crawled into their sleeping bags and passed out in the back of the truck.

Dawson stuck his hand and his head out of the sleeping bag so he could see his watch. Six-thirty. He'd gotten a big two and a half hours of sleep.

Gee, what a swell adventure this was turning out to be.

He climbed out of his sleeping bag and nudged Pacey with his foot. Pacey just snored louder. Dawson nudged him again, harder this time.

"I'm sick I can't go to school let me sleep," Pacey mumbled, turning over.

Great.

The lights went on inside the McDonald's. Dawson's stomach rumbled hungrily. He picked up his video camera and scrambled out of the truck, his breath coming in puffs from the cold.

"Good-morning-welcome-to-McDonald's-can-I-take-your-order-please," a short girl with big hair behind the counter asked in a bored monotone. She clicked her gum and waited.

Dawson ordered coffee and two muffins, ate the muffins quickly, and went back outside with the coffee. Maybe the cold air combined with the coffee would wake him up.

Cars pulled into the parking lot. People went inside the restaurant for breakfast. A line of cars quickly formed at the drive-through. An old blue Mustang convertible pulled in and caught his attention. For one thing, cold as it was, the top was down. And for another, the girl behind the wheel was sensational-looking.

She had straight blond hair tied back with a ribbon. With her was a little boy with red hair and freckles. She parked and they got out of the car. Now he saw what she was wearing—black leggings and an oversized sweater. Even though she walked with her toes kind of turned out, there was an awesome grace about her.

"I want a milk shake!" the little boy yelled, jumping around with excitement.

"It's breakfast, Tommy," the girl said. Her voice had a soft, southern twang to it. "Don't you want a muffin or some eggs?"

"You said everything I wanted I could have! The top down, a milk shake, and an ice cream cone for dessert!"

I wonder if she's his au pair, Dawson thought. He'd already been down that road the previous summer, when he'd met Sheila. But this girl was light-years more beautiful than Sheila. Not only that, but every time she moved, it was as if she was floating. Poetry in motion.

"I know I did, but your momma will kill me if I—"

"Milk shake! Milk shake! Milk shake!" Tommy chanted at the top of his lungs.

"Dang, quit yelling!" the girl said. "If you promise to hush, you can have ten milk shakes."

"Yeaaaaaahhhh!" Tommy cheered.

Dawson was mesmerized. He loved everything about her, from her soft accent to the funny, graceful way she walked, to promising the kid he could have the top down on the car.

She knelt down to the little boy and zipped up his jacket. Then she tied his shoe. Impetuously, Dawson lifted the camera and aimed it at her. She turned and looked at him, cocking her head to one side on her long, slender neck. Then she took Tommy's hand and walked over to him.

"What are you doin'?" she asked softly.

"Filming you," Dawson said. "You just looked so . . . you're very graceful. I hope you don't mind." He lowered the camera and looked at her.

"No," the girl said. "And thanks for the compliment. Sayin' that I'm graceful, I mean."

"Let's go, Dixie!" the little boy yelled. "Milk shake!"

"Hush," she told him. She looked at Dawson again. "So, do you live around here?"

"No." He lifted the camera again and began to film her as he spoke. "I live quite a ways from here. My friend and I—he's in the truck over there— drove in last night to visit some friends."

"I'm Dixie," the girl said, sticking her hand out.

Dawson switched the camera to his left hand and shook with her. Her hand was small and soft, and, in spite of the cold, warm. "Dawson," he said.

She gave him a shy smile. "Dawson. I like that."

"Weren't you cold with the top down?" Dawson asked her.

She laughed. "It was Tommy's idea. Today is his birthday—"

"I'm six," Tommy piped up.

"—and I told him he got to pick everything he wanted," she finished. "So, top down."

"It was fun," Tommy said. "I wasn't cold."

She smiled at the kid. "Me, neither."

Tommy pulled on Dixie's hand. "Let's go now!"

"Thomas Joseph, you be a gentleman," she chided him.

"Yuck." But he stopped tugging.

Dixie smiled at Dawson again. "My nephew. I'm just here visiting from Mississippi. Ever been?"

Dawson shook his head no.

"I came up for an audition with the City Ballet. I've been studying forever."

"Did you get in?" Dawson asked.

She shook her head no sadly. "Shot down. But I guess I'll try again next year." She got a faraway look in her eyes. "All I ever wanted to be is a dancer." She focused on him again. "Want to see me dance?"

Before Dawson could say anything, the girl—Dixie—had dropped Tommy's arm and gracefully raised her hands over her head. Then she began to dance. She swirled and swayed, leaped and twirled to music only she could hear. Dawson got it all on camera. Finally her hands fluttered back to her sides, and she stopped.

"That was beyond incredible," Dawson said. He put the camera down.

Her face lit up. "Really?"

"Really."

"Thanks. Bein' the best dancer in Jackson, Mississippi isn't—well, what you said means a lot to me. After gettin' shot down and all."

"You're going to be so famous one day," Dawson said fervently. "I know it."

She scuffed one sneaker into the cement of the parking lot. "Sometimes it feels stupid to have a dream."

Something gave way in Dawson's heart. "It isn't. A dream is ... it's everything. No one can take it away from you. All great people began with nothing more than a dream."

She gave him a radiant smile. "Yeah. I like that."

"*Now* can we go, Dixie?" Tommy said, reaching for her hand again.

"Yeah, sweetie," she told him. "You were a real gentleman too, Tommy Joseph." She turned back to Dawson. "Well, it was nice to meet you." She turned away.

"Wait!" Dawson cried. He couldn't just let her go. "Are you—I mean—what are you doing later?" he blurted out.

"Taking dance class," Dixie said.

"After that?" Dawson persisted. He didn't know where the nerve came from.

"After that is Tommy's birthday party. And after that, well, I'm going back to Mississippi tomorrow."

Dawson didn't know what to say. But it just felt so tragic to think that he'd never see her again.

"I guess we're just ships that pass in the night. Well, the day, anyway," she amended, giving him that golden smile again. She reached for his hand. "Goodbye, Dawson. Thanks for—well, just thanks."

He watched her walk her funny duckwalk into McDonald's, too upset to even lift the camera to film her.

"Hey." Pacey stood there, blinking sleepily.

"How is it that you can meet someone, purely by chance, and in the briefest of encounters they can touch you so deeply that you feel a profound loss at the thought of never seeing them again?" Dawson asked.

"Okay, I'm filling in the blanks here," Pacey said.

"My guess is—call me crazy—you met a girl. A babe. And said babe has already passed in and out of your life."

"She's in there," Dawson said, cocking his head toward the restaurant.

"Cool," Pacey said. "Let's go in and do the breakfast thing, you can hook up with the babe while I look up Jen's address in a Manhattan directory."

"No," Dawson said sadly. "If I see her again and then lose her again, I'll feel even worse."

"Well, I'm gonna go in and use the john, get some food, and get Jen's address," Pacey said, yawning. "You coming or not?"

"Not. I'll wait in the truck."

"Dawson, cheer up and try to follow my logic. You met a babe. There are an infinite number of babes in this world. The best one could be around the very next corner. This babe is but one in an infinite series of babe possibilities." Pacey clapped Dawson on the shoulder, then went into the restaurant.

Dawson went back to the truck. He hoped they would leave before Dixie left the restaurant. He'd rather have a perfect memory of her than have to watch her walk away again. At least he'd recorded her forever on videotape.

With a start, he realized something. He had completely forgotten about Joey. And Joey was the reason he was sitting in a parking lot in Staten Island. Which meant if it hadn't been for Joey, he never would have met Dixie.

Which was way too weird to figure out on two and a half hours of sleep.

Chapter 12

"This is dee-lish," Joey said, as she buttered her third slice of the thick, yellow bread and took a huge bite. "What's it called again? Challah?"

Jen laughed. "Not chah-lah, like chew. Challah, like you're clearing your throat. It's a New York thing. Try it."

"Challah." It came out exactly the same way.

"You can take the girl out of Capeside," Jen joked, "but you can't take—"

"Yeah, yeah." Joey grinned, taking another huge bite. "It's awesome. In fact, all this food is to die for. Of course, I would basically feel that way about any cuisine that did not involve me serving it."

They were having lunch at Kiev, a funky Ukrainian restaurant in the funky East Village. So far Joey had tried borscht, a cold beet soup; pierogis, moon-shaped dumplings with mashed potatoes inside; and a delicious dish made up of bow-tie noodles with some kind of nutty grain, all covered in brown sauce. And of course, the incredible bread with the unpronounceable name. They were on their second basketful.

The night before they'd fallen asleep quickly—it was after two by the time they got back to Jen's. Joey had woken up early, full of energy. She wanted to make the most of every single minute she had in New York. Even the evil eye of Mrs. Richardson couldn't dampen her mood. So what if Danny had turned out to be an idiot? She had loved the adventure of it anyway. So just bring on some more, was her motto for the rest of her weekend.

They ordered up breakfast from the coffee shop across the street from Jen's building—Joey had loved that. Then they'd gone to the Statue of Liberty and climbed to the top, and then Joey had wanted to go to the Empire State Building. Jen had tried to convince Joey that they should go to the World Trade Center instead, since it was newer and higher, but Joey was adamant. She'd wanted to go to the Empire State Building ever since she'd seen *Sleepless in Seattle* and *An Affair to Remember*.

It had been freezing on the observation deck, but Joey had just stood there, her hair blowing around her face, tourists from all over the world bustling past her, tingling with happiness. She was Meg Ryan waiting for Tom Hanks. Anything could happen. Anything at all.

"So, what do Ukrainians eat for dessert?" Joey asked Jen, as she swallowed the last of the challah.

"You really have room?" Jen asked, incredulous.

"Sure," Joey said cheerfully. "Besides, when will I ever get to eat Ukrainian again?"

"Actually, they're famous here for the rice pudding."

Joey's face changed. "I haven't had that since . . ."

"Since when?"

"My mom used to make it," she said quietly. "Maybe I don't have room for dessert after all. So, what's next?"

"We hop in a cab and go down to lower Broadway," Jen said, whipping out her credit card to pay the check. "And then we shop till we drop." The plump Ukrainian waitress took away the card and the check.

"My funds range between extremely limited and nonexistent," Joey said self-consciously. Each time Jen paid for something, she felt a little more embarrassed. And Jen paid for everything.

"We can just walk around and look," Jen said.

They got a taxi quickly, but the driver barely spoke English, and even though Jen kept yelling that he was going the wrong way, he took them crosstown to run up the meter before he took them downtown.

"They love to pull that scam. No tip for him," Jen said when they got out of the taxi.

The wind had died down, the sun now shone brightly, it had warmed up a lot. It was as if the storm of the night before had never happened. Joey wore Jen's leather motorcycle jacket over a long-sleeved thermal T-shirt and jeans. Jen wore an old flannel shirt with a ripped collar under a cropped cotton sweater, jeans, and a New York Yankees baseball cap.

Joey couldn't help wondering if Jen had dressed down to make her feel more comfortable. Well, if she did, it's working, Joey thought, as they crossed the street and turned onto Broadway.

"You ladies are as fine as wine," a skinny street guy in filthy clothes said, bowing to them elegantly. They kept walking, and the guy walked with them. "Could you ladies perhaps spare a dime, a quarter, or whatever to help out a hungry man in his time of need?"

Joey reached into her purse and felt around for change. She handed him whatever she came up with.

"God bless you, sweet thing," he said, bowing. He began to hit up the couple walking behind them.

The street scene was fantastic and crowded, mostly young, and oh-so-hip. There were people of every color, most of them were wearing black clothes.

Vendors lined the sidewalk close to the busy street, selling sunglasses, socks, incense and jewelry. There were art galleries and used clothing stores. And boutiques so exclusive they only had two or three items in their pristine window displays.

"Come and look, pretty girls," a vendor called to them. He had smooth, dark skin and spoke with a lilting singsong. "I give you very good price."

They just smiled and walked by.

Joey stopped in front of a display of silver jewelry that looked different from the others. She picked up a delicate silver ring with a moon, a sun, and a star in the center. She tried it on and waggled her fingers.

"Pretty," Jen said.

"It suits you," the handsome vendor told her. "All my jewelry is one of a kind. I don't make any two alike."

Joey was surprised. "You're the artist? I thought you just sold the stuff."

He smiled. "I do both. That's the first ring I made after my girlfriend gave birth to our daughter last month, so I have a soft spot for it. I call it a dream ring."

Joey looked at the tiny white tag with the price on it. Twenty-two dollars. It was almost all the money she had with her. I'm not going to go home empty-handed, she told herself. When I wear this ring, I'll always remember my very first trip to New York.

"I'll take it," Joey said. She counted out the money and handed it to him.

He handed Joey her change and smiled. "May all your dreams come true."

"Thanks," Joey said, smiling back at him. "Really." She admired her ring as they walked along.

"Oh, let's go in here," Jen said, "it's a hoot."

The store was called Truly, Madly, Deeply. Loud rock music blasted through the sound system. The first thing Joey saw was a hot pink latex dress with the breasts cut out, trimmed in hot pink feathers.

"Who would wear something like that?" Joey asked.

"Someone who is truly, madly, deeply desperate for attention." Jen held up a tiny transparent plastic skirt covered with handpainted daisies.

"It's so *you*," Joey teased her. She wandered through the store, looking at this and that, almost backing into a nude mannequin draped in nothing but a feather boa. She checked the price tag on a tie-dyed cotton minidress. A hundred and eighty dollars. She dropped it quickly.

"I actually like this," Jen said, holding up a black lace minidress layered over baby-blue chiffon. "What do you think?"

Joey shrugged. "I'm a jeans and T-shirt kind of girl."

"I'm gonna try it on." Jen disappeared into one of the tiny stalls. The door only covered her from midthigh to shoulder level. But it didn't really matter, because the door was entirely transparent.

"Uh, Jen?" Joey called. "Everyone out here can see everything."

"Watch this," Jen said. She flipped the lock. Instantly Joey could no longer see through the door.

"Amazing," Joey marveled. "I mean, I don't see the point, but still, it's amazing."

A gaunt salesman dressed in black approached Joey. He wore eye makeup. Both his ears were pierced, with large, gold hoops in them. He looked Joey up and down. "Can I help you?" His voice dripped disdain.

"My friend is in there," Joey said quickly, feeling flustered. "I mean, she's trying something on."

"Just scream for Roberto if you need help," he

said. "I'm not Roberto, of course, but I do like the name." He wafted away.

Jen came out in the dress. "What do you think?" She peered at herself in a three-way mirror.

Joey's confidence took a nosedive.

Because Jen looked, in a word, perfect.

"It looks great," Joey told her.

"You think?" Jen turned her back to the mirror to check out her butt. "I don't look fat?"

"Please Jen, don't turn into one of those girls with a great body who insists that she's fat, I'm begging you."

Jen laughed. "Back in New York for twenty-four hours and I'm already falling back into all the old head games. I think I'll buy this."

Jen handed the dress to the salesman who was not named Roberto. Joey glanced at the amount printed on the credit card slip. Two hundred and sixty-five dollars. Plus tax. And Jen hadn't thought about it twice.

Joey tried not to resent it. It wasn't like Jen threw it in her face or anything. And Jen was being so nice about taking Joey to the touristy places, and treating her to everything.

Because I can't afford to pay for anything, Joey thought glumly. It is just so unfair.

"I think I'll wear this dress tonight," Jen said as they pushed out the door and strolled down lower Broadway. "It will make my aunt insane."

"Why?" Joey asked.

"Because Courtney's sweet sixteen is formal."

Joey looked at her blankly.

"You know. The guys wear black tie and the girls wear long gowns," Jen translated.

"Oh, yeah, right," Joey said, nodding. "I've gone to, like, a million of those." A scary feeling fluttered through her stomach. "Unfortunately, though, I left my formal collection at Buckingham Palace, last time I was hanging with the queen. She's crazed to fix me up with Prince William, by the way."

Jen bumped her hip into Joey playfully. "I've got the perfect dress you can borrow. Don't worry."

"I wasn't," Joey lied. They walked for a while, looking in shop windows. Joey cleared her throat. "This perfect dress would be long, correct?"

"Correct."

"But long on you would be midcalf on me."

"This dress will be long on you," Jen assured her. "Because—"

"Don't tell me," Joey interrupted. "You never got a chance to shorten it."

"Right."

"Why, if it isn't Jen Lindley," a girl getting out of a taxi cooed. She was small and thin, with perfectly streaked brown hair framing her pinched features. Over jeans and black velvet shirt her mink coat, dyed blue, flapped open. "Long time no see and blah, blah, blah."

Jen's face went stony. She'd known Miranda Briarly just about all of her life, and she'd loathed her for an equal amount of time. Miranda lived to spread rumors, the nastier the better, and she'd spread many a rumor about Jen. The problem was, about half of the vicious rumors she told were actually true.

"Hi, Miranda."

Miranda shook her hair off her face. "I heard a nasty little rumor that you were going to show your face at Courtney's party tonight."

"You know how much I love nasty little rumors," Jen said.

Miranda laughed. "That's because they're usually about you. How was rehab?"

"*What?*" Jen asked.

"I heard you were in rehab for . . . well, it doesn't matter, if it isn't true." Her eyes flitted across Joey. "And you would be—?"

"And you would be—?" Joey shot back.

"Miranda Briarly," the girl said. "Jen and I go way back."

"Joelle Potter."

"Potter, Potter, do we know any Potters?" Miranda mused. "What do your people do?"

Joey shrugged. "The usual. Have babies out of wedlock. Go to prison on felony charges. Whatever."

Jen snorted back a laugh.

"Aren't you amusing," Miranda oozed. "Well, must run. I've got to get a manicure and a facial before tonight." She hesitated. "I don't know if I should tell you—"

"Right," Jen said. "You shouldn't. Let's go, Joe—Joelle." They started to walk away.

"I think you'll want to know about this before tonight," Miranda called.

Jen turned around, resigned. "What?" she snapped.

"It's about Billy. And your cousin Courtney."

Jen just stood there waiting.

"Well, in case you haven't heard," Miranda said slowly, "they've been seeing each other for months. In fact, they're practically living together." Her mouth curled into a cold smile. "I knew you'd want to know."

Chapter 13

Dawson ate the last bite of his hot dog and leaned back on the bench, watching the Rangers fans scurrying into Madison Square Garden. Rodents of civilization, he thought. It will never, ever, ever be me. I will become a famous filmmaker, and I will do great, important things.

Or, I will kill Pacey and gladly face the death penalty. Because so far he has managed to screw this trip up every single step of the way.

That morning, at the McDonald's in Staten Island, Pacey had discovered a crucial New York City fact—no one outside of Manhattan had a Manhattan phone book. So they came up with a plan: drive into Manhattan, park the truck, and find a phone book.

Some plan. Dawson got directions into Manhattan, that part came off without a hitch. But getting from lower Manhattan to Times Square—where Pacey wanted to go, since he saw it on television every New Year's Eve—took forever.

It was as if the traffic was reproducing; it just kept getting worse. People crossed the street in front of them and behind them, blithely ignoring the DON'T WALK signs. Kids on in-line skates and skateboards whizzed by.

They kept getting gridlocked. As in not moving at all. A half hour behind a jackknifed tractor-trailer. An hour in a traffic jam caused by a broken water main. Another half hour due to construction.

But finally they made it to Times Square, only to find that parking in a lot near there cost a small fortune. The next hour was spent trying, in vain, to find a parking spot on the street. Finally Pacey maneuvered the truck between a taxi stand and a fire hydrant, on a deserted-looking block so far west it was practically in the Hudson River.

They walked to Times Square, asking in every restaurant and every tourist trap if they had a phone directory. They might as well have been asking for the Holy Grail. Either no one in New York possessed a Manhattan phone book, or else no one was giving said phone book to them.

Finally, Dawson had come up with the brilliant notion that Pennsylvania Station would have phone booths and directories. After all, it was full of travelers from out of town catching trains. They got directions from a cute girl, and hoofed it there, getting caught in an unruly mob heading to the hockey game at Madison Square Garden.

Excellent. Phone booths. Phone directories. Now

all they had to do was find Jen's address and phone number. Lindley. But what was Jen's father's name? And who knew there were dozens of Lindleys in the Manhattan phone book?

Dawson eyed the bank of phone booths across from him, where Pacey was trying yet another Lindley on the list. They had hit answering machines, no answers, busy signals, disconnected numbers, little kids, and adults. What they had not hit was one single soul who had ever heard of Jennifer Lindley, currently residing in Capeside.

Just as Dawson was debating the purchase of another hot dog, Pacey came over to him. "No luck. We need more change."

Dawson pointed in the direction of the newsstand.

"Have a heart," Pacey whined. "He hates me. Last time I asked for change he cursed my mother in Hindi."

"How do you know?" Dawson asked.

"He translated." Pacey thrust a ten-dollar bill at Dawson. "My last tenspot, so guard it with your life."

Dawson went to the newsstand and smiled at the Indian vendor, who eyed him and his video camera suspiciously.

"A roll of these mints, and could I have all the change in quarters, please?" Dawson asked, handing over the ten.

A stream of Hindi flew from the vendor's lips. "I am not a bank, young man!" he added in lilting English.

"Right," Dawson agreed. "But if you could just

spare as many quarters as you can, I would be very grateful."

The vendor humphed his anger, but he turned to his cash box and began to count out quarters. Dawson lifted his camera to film the crowd in the train station while he waited. A little girl and her mother in matching dresses, both carrying red balloons. A couple kissing. A businessman surreptitiously picking his nose. Ugh—zoom off of that. A beautiful blond girl who walked with her toes turned out—

Dixie! He was sure it was her. She had just gotten on the escalator, which led up to the street. He wanted to run after her. But they were so low on funds, he couldn't leave the ten dollars with the vendor.

"Can I have that change quickly?" Dawson asked, eyeing the escalator.

"You should be patient, young man," the vendor said, cracking open a fresh roll of quarters. "I am only doing this for you out of the goodness of my heart."

"I'll just take the ten back, then." Dawson held out his hand, craning his neck to try and see Dixie on the escalator. Come on, come on, come on!

The vendor eyed him. "You are a sorry excuse for a human being. You must buy more than mints for my trouble. And then I will give you change. But not," he added, folding his arms, "in quarters."

A beat, as Dawson's eyes slid from the vendor to the escalator. To the ten-dollar bill. Without allowing himself to think, he grabbed the money and ran for the escalator. From behind him, Dawson heard the vendor yelling in Hindi, and Pacey yelling in English.

Dawson ran up the escalator and looked both ways. No sign of Dixie. He ran outside, onto Seventh Avenue. There were so many people, all hurrying somewhere or other.

Pacey ran up to him. "What was that about?"

Dawson's spirits sagged. "She's gone."

"Who's gone?"

"Her. Dixie. The girl from this morning. I saw her, but I lost her."

"Mirage," Pacey said. "Your mind playing tricks on you. Also known as wishful thinking."

"No," Dawson said. "It was her."

"If you say so, *compadre*." Pacey grabbed the ten-dollar bill from Dawson's hand. "This is about to translate into more hot dogs—love those push-carts. You?"

Dawson shook his head no. They walked over to the hot dog vendor. Dawson's mind was still on Dixie. "I can't believe I let her get away again."

Pacey paid the vendor and took a huge bite out of his onion-topped hot dog. "You seem to have already forgotten Pacey's Theory of Babe Relativity." Mustard dribbled down his chin.

"What if you're wrong?" Dawson asked him. "What if in fact there is only one perfect soul mate out there for each of us? And if we get lucky enough to meet that soul mate, we have a responsibility to make a true connection, or risk spending our entire lives yearning for something we didn't even realize we had?"

Pacey cocked an eye at him. "And what if there's another babe around the corner?"

Dawson sighed. "Wipe your chin."

Pacey complied. "Let Doctor P. give you a little lesson in human nature, Dawson. You want Joey. Joey does not want you. You feel rejected. You meet Dixie, a babe. You project onto said babe characteristics that make you think she is your soul mate. This you do out of your massive insecurity due to rejection by said Joey."

"And I suppose it's your wealth of experience with women that leads you to this conclusion," Dawson said.

"I have a sensational love life," Pacey replied. "Unfortunately, the vast majority of it takes place with paper partners."

"You realize that we're not going to find Jen's address."

Pacey popped the last bite of hot dog into his mouth. "That thought had crossed my mind. However, I have already come up with plan B."

"Plan B," Dawson repeated. "So far your plan A has been a one hundred percent failure."

"Which is why plan B will look so excellent in comparison," Pacey said. "Can you spell 'crash,' boys and girls?"

Dawson looked at him blankly.

"This much we know: the sweet sixteen is at the Plaza Hotel," Pacey said. "There can't be more than one sweet sixteen there tonight for a girl named Courtney."

"Probably true," Dawson allowed.

"Definitely true. And what sweet sixteen wouldn't

welcome two manly men such as ourselves?" He
clapped Dawson on the back. "I know a few things
have gone wrong. But from now on it's going to be
smooth sailing. Just let Captain Pacey set the course.
Tonight, my man, we cruise into party mode, full
steam ahead."

"Somehow that does not fill me with confidence."

"Trust me, Dawson. We have reached a dead end
on the ol' problem highway. Of that I am sure."

Doug Witter parked his police car in a no-parking
zone in front of the Ice House—one advantage of
being a cop was that you never got a ticket—and
went inside. The place was hopping, but then, it
usually was on a Saturday afternoon.

"Hi, Bessie," Doug said, taking a seat at the
counter. "Just a quick coffee and a couple of
those doughnuts."

Across the room, Abby Morgan sat with Nellie
Olson, flirting with some cute guys from the University of Massachusetts who were sitting at the next
table.

"So, what do you do for fun in this town?" one
guy asked.

"It's so provincial here," Nellie said, shaking her
curls. "But we're up for anything. Right, Abby?"

Abby wasn't paying any attention. Her eyes were
glued to Doug Witter's back. She distinctly remembered Pacey saying that his brother and his father
would be at some police convention thing all weekend, which was how Pacey was able to steal their
truck. So why was Doug sitting in the Ice House
on Saturday afternoon?

"Ab?" Nellie called. "Yoo-hoo!"

"Be right back." Abby got up and crossed the room. She took a seat at the counter next to Doug, pretending to look nonchalant. Then she pretended to notice him. "Say, aren't you Pacey Witter's brother?"

Doug nodded.

"I see who got all the looks in the family," Abby said.

"Thanks." Doug smiled and took a bite of his doughnut.

"Oh, I'm so rude," Abby admonished herself. "Where are my manners? I'm Abby Morgan. I go to school with Pacey."

"Doug," Doug said. "Nice to meet you."

"Pacey talks about you all the time," Abby said. "Really. You must be his idol or something."

"I doubt that," Doug said, polishing off his doughnut.

"No, really!" Abby insisted. "Like just yesterday at school, he told me how proud he was that you and your dad were going to some police convention this weekend."

"Dad's there," Doug said. "I came back early—just got back, in fact. I haven't even been home yet. Two officers here went down with the flu. Had to come back and take over their shift. Can't have Capeside unprotected from the criminal elements."

"See, that's just the way Pacey described you," Abby gushed. "So concerned for everyone else. Like how you talked your dad into letting Pacey borrow the truck for the weekend—"

"Come again?" Doug asked.

"Pacey told me how you talked your dad into letting him take the truck this weekend," Abby explained. "You know. So that he and Dawson could go to the Nightshade concert in Albany."

Doug's face began to turn an angry red.

"Is something wrong?" Abby asked innocently.

"Why that little . . ." Doug threw some money on the counter. "Excuse me." He hurried out of the Ice House.

Bessie picked up his check and his money, and watched Doug practically run out of the restaurant. "He rushing to the scene of a crime or something?"

Abby smiled. "Oh, you might say that." She looked down at Doug's plate. He'd left one doughnut untouched. She picked it up and took a dainty bite.

No sense letting it go to waste.

Chapter 14

Gale Leery paced with the portable phone in her hand. Her head was spinning. She and Mitch had been having such a great Saturday, just lying around the house. Mitch had left just a few minutes ago to pick up a pizza for dinner. And then the phone had rung.

It was Doug Witter, Pacey's older brother. Dawson was not at Pacey's house for the weekend. Pacey wasn't even at Pacey's house. In fact, Pacey and Dawson had stolen Mr. Witter's truck and driven it to Albany, New York, of all places. To a rock concert.

"But . . . are you sure, Doug?" Gale asked. "Dawson is the most honest, trustworthy—"

"I'm sorry to say that my little brother is a terrible influence on your son, Mrs. Leery," Doug said.

"Oh, Pacey's a good kid," Gale insisted.

"I guess you just don't know him very well then, ma'am," Doug said.

Gale winced at the "ma'am" thing. It made her sound so *old*. "You can call me Gale."

"This is official police business, so I'm afraid I have to respect the formalities," Doug said.

"Official police . . . what are you talking about?"

"Stolen property," Doug said. "Actually, crossing state lines with stolen property, I might add, which could add a federal count to the charges."

"You mean because they took your dad's truck?" Gale asked, incredulous. "Is that what you're talking about?"

"Yes, ma'am. I'll be calling my father as soon as I get off the phone with you. He may want to swear out a warrant—"

"Oh, come on, Doug, that's ridiculous—"

"No, ma'am, it is not. I have a feeling that Pacey is never going to change unless he gets good and scared. It's called tough love."

Gale felt desperate, she had to do something, say something, to stop this. "How did you find out about this, Doug?"

"A witness."

"Who? Maybe the person isn't reliable."

"The witness had no reason to lie, Mrs. Leery. She's a friend of Pacey's."

"What are you planning to do now?" Gale asked.

"Call my father. Then we'll see if there's a way to track them down. I'm sorry to be the bearer of bad tidings, ma'am. I'll call you as soon as I know anything at all."

He hung up and took a piece of paper from his

back pocket. The phone number of the hotel where the law enforcement convention was being held. Quickly he dialed the number.

A good son had to do what a good son had to do.

As for Dawson's mom, she just stood there in the family room in a state of shock, the dead phone in her hand.

"I'm telling you, it's not true," Jen told Joey for maybe the twentieth time. "Billy is not involved with Courtney."

During the entire taxi ride uptown from lower Broadway, Jen had done a monologue about how Billy couldn't stand Courtney, and how Miranda was the kind of witch who knew exactly what lie to tell to freak you out.

"What I don't understand is why it would freak you out if you don't want to be with Billy anyway," Joey said.

"I don't want to be with him . . . not like I was with him before," Jen said, struggling to explain.

"You mean you want to be friends? Like me and Dawson?"

"Maybe."

Joey shrugged. "You're the one who told me that Dawson and I couldn't go from friendship to romance and then back to friendship."

Jen peered out the cab's side window. "The difference is, Billy and I were never friends in the first place."

The knowledge of that made her sad. But that was what happened when you lusted for someone so much that you never really got to know them. And they never really got to know you, either.

The driver pulled over in front of Jen's apartment building, and the doorman opened the door for them even as Jen paid the fare.

"How come we never take the subway?" Joey asked, as Jen stuffed her change carelessly into her purse.

Jen shrugged. "Habit."

"Good afternoon, Miss Lindley," the other doorman said, nodding politely, as they strode through the lobby toward the elevators.

"Someday I'm going to live in New York," Joey said. "I'll eat Chinese food every day. And Ukrainian. I'll buy my clothes at Truly, Madly, Deeply. I'll go to that bar where all the movie stars go— what's the name of it?—the one where the girls dance on the bar and leave their bras behind?"

"Heifers, I think. I went there with Billy once," Jen said. They got on the elevator. "It was wild."

"So, did you do it?" Joey asked.

"Dance on the bar and leave my bra behind?"

Joey nodded.

"I don't remember."

Because you were drinking back then, Joey realized. And you don't remember because you were wasted.

Jen unlocked the apartment door, took two steps in, and stood there in shock. Because the entire living room was full of flowers.

They were everywhere. Vases of brilliantly hued blossoms sat on every available surface. More tall vases holding long-stemmed blossoms sat on the floor. And there were rose petals all over the gleaming wood floor surrounding the tapestry white-on-white area rug.

"Wow," Joey said. "Somebody robbed a florist."

"Or spent a fortune," Jen said. "This is amazing."

"They have to be from Billy. Which means you were right about Miranda, and he wants you back truly, deeply, and might I add, madly."

On the white marble side table sat a small white card, propped up against a crystal vase of red and pink roses.

"You really should go back to him," Joey said, sniffing some exotic-looking blossoms in a black vase as Jen read the card. "This sort of extravagance should be rewarded."

"They're not from Billy," Jen said.

Joey stared at her. And then she realized. They had to be from Dawson. To make me jealous? she wondered. Or because he really wants Jen back?

"And they're not for me," Jen added.

Oh my god. Dawson had sent *her* flowers.

He must have gotten Jen's New York address from her grandmother, Joey realized. And these flowers must have cost him every penny he ever made at Screenplay.

She thought back to last year, when she had wanted him so desperately that she hurt inside all the time, because Jen had him and she didn't. And now. Now that they weren't together, he did this. It was so . . . so Dawson. To do the most incredibly sensitive right thing at the most incredibly wrong time.

"I'm beginning to think that there is something to

the theory that men lust for the chase," Joey said. "Dawson never did anything remotely like this when we were a couple. But now that we're not a couple, he—"

"Joey," Jen interrupted, "they're not from Dawson." She held out the card.

Joey read it. "Dear Joelle," she read aloud. "The only thing greater than my stupidity is your beauty. I was an idiot last night. Can I make it up to you? Danny."

She looked up at Jen. "This has to be a joke, right?"

"I have no idea," Jen said, shrugging.

"But, but . . . I hated him," Joey sputtered, looking at the card again. "And he hated me. And . . . this is extremely weird."

"Hello, girls," Mrs. Richardson said in a nasal voice. She stood in the hallway rubbing her red-rimmed eyes. She blew her nose into a lace hankie. "I see you got the delivery."

"Who could miss it?" Jen asked.

Mrs. Richardson sneezed. "I'm terribly allergic to most flowers," she said, blowing her nose again. "This is torture for me."

"You could leave," Jen suggested innocently.

"So that you can have young people up here against the wishes of your parents?" Mrs. Richardson asked.

"Well, basically, yeah," Jen replied.

Mrs. Richardson ignored that. "By the way, your parents called while you were out. They said Courtney's birthday present is in the blue box in the china cabinet. And I was to remind you to give Courtney's parents their regrets for their not having attended."

"Present. Regrets. Got it." Jen turned to Joey. "This is so perfectly my parents. Why put yourself out when simply buying something extravagant will suffice?"

"They also asked how you were conducting yourself," Mrs. Richardson added.

"You didn't tell them about the orgy, did you?" Jen asked.

"I told them the truth," the older woman said. "Other than being extremely rude to me, you hadn't done anything untoward at all." She sneezed again. "I'll be in my room. And you can be as rude as you like, Miss Lindley, I'm not leaving." She strode down the hall.

"Hey, hang in there, fight the good fight!" Jen called after her. She turned to Joey. "This is crazy. I'm actually kind of starting to like her."

The antique phone on the coffee table rang, she picked it up. "Hello?"

"Hi, Jen? Danny Fields."

"Somehow I don't think you called to talk to me. Hold on." She held out the phone to Joey.

"Who?" Joey asked, taking the phone. She put it to her ear. "Hello?"

"Joelle."

Danny. He had said her name—well, the name she had invented, anyway—like it was a prayer.

She had no idea what to say to him. "Hi." She winced. Hi. How sophisticated.

"Did you get my little present?" Danny asked.

"Jen's living room looks like the Rose Bowl parade."

He laughed. "I figured you'd gotten flowers from guys so many times that I needed to make a grand gesture to stand out from the crowd."

"How very *Pretty Woman*," Joey quipped sarcastically.

"Pardon me?"

"Julia Roberts? Richard Gere? He spends significant money on her, and in return she gives him—"

"That's not why I did it," Danny said into the phone.

"No?"

"No. And besides, Julia Roberts was poor. A prostitute. You're rich. And you had the class to both turn me down *and* tell me off last night."

Joey paced with the phone. "So, I abused you and you liked it, is that it?"

Danny laughed. "You'd be surprised how many girls don't respect themselves, Joelle. I just really wanted to apologize, and to make it up to you. I was wondering if I could take you to dinner before Courtney's party?"

"No," Joey said bluntly. "Look—"

"Wait, wait, don't hang up," Danny said quickly. "Can I at least escort you to the party? I've got the limo."

Right. Like a big car was going to make her change her mind. "Gee, let me think about it. Okay, I've thought about it. No."

"I'm not giving up, Joelle."

"Hey, may the force be with you." She hung up the phone.

"What did he do, offer to buy you the Hope Diamond?" Jen asked.

"Just dinner and a ride to the party in Dad's limo."

Jen grinned. "You were exceedingly great with him just now."

Joey flushed at the compliment. It wasn't like she had so much experience with guys that she knew what she was doing, because she definitely did not. "Jen he . . . for some reason, he thinks I'm rich."

"Because he met you with me, I guess," Jen said. "All those kids are. Well, none of their parents are hurting for money. Does it bother you?"

"No. I just wish it was true."

"Money isn't everything, Joey."

Joey flushed with anger. "Do you have any idea how obnoxious it is when rich people say that? Do you have any idea how it makes someone like me feel?"

Jen thought a minute. "You're right."

"I am?"

Jen nodded. "I take money for granted. It's not fair."

Joey folded her arms. "How am I supposed to get all self-righteous and indignant if you give in that easily?"

"You're not," Jen said. "Now, can we get back to the subject at hand, namely Danny I-Want-You-So-Desperately-I-Could-Die Fields? I say we make sure that you look so incredible tonight that he is drooling for you."

"So that I can stomp on his shallow, self-involved, conquest-driven, tiny little whatever-organ-I-choose?"

"Exactly." Jen reached for Joey's hand and pulled her toward the bedroom. "Let's go play makeover. Cinderella is going to the ball!"

Chapter 15

Jen and Joey stood side by side, checking out their reflections in the floor-length mirror on the double doors of Jen's closet.

"I have to hand it to you, Cinderella," Jen told Joey's reflection, "you clean up nice. Just like for the beauty contest."

Joey nodded thoughtfully. "It's amazing what two hours of intense primping—not to mention a small fortune's worth of clothes, cosmetics, and accessories—can accomplish."

Joey wore a long, formfitting, Asian-inspired red satin gown with a tiny Mandarin collar and a slit up one leg, courtesy of Jen's closet. Her hair was up, courtesy of Jen's styling, with just a few sexy tendrils hanging down around her face. Her ears sparkled with ruby studs, courtesy of Jen's jewelry box. Her eyes were lined with smoky black eyeliner. Her lipstick was as red as her dress.

Next to her, Jen had on the dress she'd bought that afternoon. Her hair was piled on her head, stayed by rhinestone butterfly hairpins. Her lipstick was as pale as Joey's was dark.

"I ask you, are we hot or are we hot?" Jen queried.

"The former," Joey agreed. "As well as the latter. Lucky for me you don't remember to shorten your clothes. Just one thing, though. What do we wear over this so we don't freeze?"

"I've got a fake fur jacket you can wear." Jen rummaged through her closet and brought it out.

"You're sure it's fake?" Joey asked, as she tried on the black fur jacket. "It looks so real."

"I don't do fur, trust me," Jen said. "I might as well wear the motorcycle jacket. After all, I'll be the only girl there who isn't wearing a floor-length dress. And I do have a certain bad-girl rep to maintain."

In the elevator, Joey started to feel nervous. "There aren't any royal curtsies involved at this thing, are there?"

Jen laughed. "Courtney would like to think so, but trust me, her royalty is only in her mind."

They swept through the lobby, the doorman nodding to them appreciatively. When he rushed to open the door for them, Joey didn't feel funny at all.

"Actually, Jen, I could get used to—"

"Uh, Joey?" Jen cocked her head toward the street.

Joey looked. There at the curb was a white and gold horse-drawn carriage. The driver wore white tails and a gold top hat. And, leaning against the carriage, clad in perfect black tuxedos, were Danny and Billy.

The girls walked over to them, dumbfounded.

Danny kissed Joey's hand. "You are so hot."

"Wh . . . what is this?" Joey stammered, dazzled in spite of herself. "I mean, you said a limo. And I said no. Didn't I?"

"You did," Danny admitted.

"We were hoping we'd impress you ladies so much that you'd relent," Billy said, smiling that way-too-sexy smile at Jen. "And by the way, you look fantastic."

"So do you," Jen admitted. Why did he have to be so handsome? How did he manage to retain that rebel look in a tux? Why did she fall for it?

"Uh, excuse us." Jen pulled Joey a few feet away. "What do you want to do?"

"I don't know," Joey admitted. "I mean, I don't trust Danny. I don't want to be his date or anything, but . . ." She looked wistfully behind her. "It's just so fairy tale."

They went back over to the guys. "We'll go with you," Jen said, "on one condition."

"Which would be?" Danny asked.

"No strings," Jen said. "Understood?"

"Understood, Madame Warden," Danny said, bowing.

The driver helped them all into the carriage, covering their laps with a warm blanket. Joey couldn't help it; when the horse began to trot, she felt as if she was starring in some fantastic movie. She looked over at Danny. If only she was in love with the leading man.

"Having fun?" Danny reached for her hand.

She smiled at him; she couldn't help it. He was so gorgeous. And rich. And he was so into her. Maybe he'd just had an off night the night before. Maybe he wasn't really such a player after all.

"Yeah," Joey admitted. "This is fantastic."

"No, *you're* fantastic, Joelle." He put his arm around her. She let him. Across from them, Billy was kissing Jen. And Jen was kissing him back.

Joey felt something cold sting her forehead. She looked up. "It's snowing! Too cool!" She threw her head back, stuck out her tongue and let the snowflakes dissolve on her tongue.

"Do you have any idea how adorable you are?" Danny asked her.

"Oh, I have some idea," Joey replied. "On a one to ten adorable scale, I'm an eleven point five, easy."

"Joelle, let's pretend last night never happened," Danny said, gazing into her eyes.

"I suppose we could hire a hypnotist to erase it from our memories," Joey teased.

Danny laughed. "He can name his price. I'll do it." Gently he tipped her face to his.

"Forget last night?" Joey whispered.

He nodded, and waited. The snow danced in her hair. She was in a horse-drawn carriage in New York City, on her way to a fantastic party at a fancy hotel, where everyone would be young and rich and beautiful. And for the first time in Joey's life, she *felt* rich and beautiful. Carefree. It just felt so perfect, and she never wanted it to end.

"Joelle?" His question hung in the air.

Her kiss was all the answer he needed.

The Rose Room of the Plaza Hotel took Joey's breath away. It was huge, with crystal chandeliers and a dance floor surrounded by tables covered with snowy linen and set for ten. Along one wall there was a buffet table, in the center of the table was a huge ice sculpture. COURTNEY'S SWEET 16 was carved into the ice, surrounded by a halo of white orchids and pink roses. Next to that was a bar. An orchestra played on a raised stage. Waiters moved silently among the guests, offering champagne or soft drinks.

On one wall a continuous slide show was being presented—slide after slide of Courtney. She was a little girl playing in the snow. She was Mary in the Christmas pageant at church. She danced with her father. She posed on a beach someplace tropical.

"This is . . . amazing," Joey whispered to Jen.

"No, *that's* amazing," Jen said.

She was facing the opposite wall. Joey turned around. There was a huge oil painting—it had to be more than ten feet high—a copy of the famous *Mona Lisa*.

Only instead of Mona Lisa's face, there was Courtney's.

Joey was flabbergasted. "Is this, like, normal?" she asked Jen. "I mean, I have no basis for comparison."

"Trust me," Jen said. "Normal does not enter into it."

"Cousin Jen!" a tall, slender girl with perfectly

streaked straight blond hair headed for them, her arms opened wide. She wore a stunningly beautiful long, white lace dress with a pink underlayer, and a single strand of pearls around her graceful neck.

Has to be Courtney-the-Perfect, Joey thought, as the tall girl leaned over to air-kiss Jen in the vicinity of first one cheek, and then, as if she had been raised in France, the other.

"Hi, Courtney," Jen said. "Happy birthday."

A table in the corner piled high with brightly wrapped presents caught her eye. Oops. She'd forgotten to bring Courtney's present. "I'm having your birthday present delivered because it's . . . special."

"You're just so sweet," Courtney cooed. She looked at Joey. "And you must be Jen's little friend she said she was bringing."

"Joey," Joey told her. "Thanks for inviting me. Your dress is really beautiful," she added shyly.

"Thanks," Courtney said. "It's a Vera Wang. I had such a fight with Mother over the pink silk under the lace! She said wearing a long white gown for your sweet sixteen is a sign of breeding and purity, can you imagine?" Her eyes flitted over Jen's dress. "And you're wearing black! And it's short! But you always were daring, Jen. I'd never have the nerve!"

"Oh well, you know nervy me," Jen said.

Courtney frowned slightly. "It's a tad low-cut, Cuz. I just don't want people to get the idea that . . . well, that you haven't mended your ways."

"Actually, Courtney, I don't even have on underwear," Jen pretended to confess. "I was thinking of dancing on the buffet table. High kicks. Very Rockettes."

Courtney paled.

"It's a joke, Courtney," Jen explained. "And before you ask, I'm totally sober. Twenty-four-seven."

"I wasn't going to ask," Courtney protested.

"Sparkling cider?" Billy asked, coming up next to her. "Evidently the powers that be gave strict orders not to serve liquor to anyone underage, or I'd be offering you champagne."

"Oh, you know how my parents are," Courtney said, rolling her eyes. "But you came prepared, right, Billy?"

Billy feigned hurt. "See, this is how rumors get started."

"You're just so *bad*, Billy," Courtney slapped playfully at his arm. "What did you bring?"

Billy held out his hands. "Empty-handed."

"Oh, poo," Courtney pouted. "Well, when you score something—*anything*—come and find me, okay? My mother is driving me *insane*."

"Sure," Billy said easily.

Courtney gazed up into Billy's eyes. "You're going to dance with me later, right?"

"I wouldn't miss it, birthday girl."

"Can't wait." She kissed him lightly on the lips, then gave Jen a smug look. "Well, excuse me. I have to mingle. Have fun!" She hurried off to greet some other guests.

Jen reached for Billy's hand. "Hey, thanks for not bringing any liquor. Really."

He put his arms around her. "No prob. But you don't mind if I go score some for Courtney, do you?"

Jen gave him a scathing look. "Oh, poo."

"She still gets to you, huh?"

"The question is, Billy, does she get to *you*?" Jen asked pointedly.

"Courtney?" He made the idea sound crazy. "You know better." He sipped his cider and turned to Joey. "Where's Danny?"

"He went to see some old friend named Jack D., I think he said."

Billy thought a beat, then he laughed. "Yeah, Jack's a buddy of mine, too. Excuse me. I shall return."

Joey scratched her chin. "At the risk of sounding like I'm from Capeside, did he just go somewhere to get whiskey?"

Jen nodded. "Jack D. is Jack Daniels. And here I thought Billy came without a bottle to make me happy." Something caught Jen's eye. "Uh-oh. See that woman making a beeline for us? Courtney's mom, my Aunt Grace. Better known as the aunt from hell."

"Jennifer!" Aunt Grace grabbed Jen and did the same affected air-kiss thing. Her hair was up in a classic French twist. Diamonds sparkled on her earlobes. Her exquisite evening gown was dove-gray silk, trimmed in a deeper gray velvet.

"Hi, Aunt Grace," Jen said.

The older woman held her at arm's length. "Let me look at you." She frowned. "Have you put on weight?"

"Don't think so, Aunt Grace."

Grace wagged her finger at Jen. "You have to be constantly vigilant, young lady. Where are your parents?"

"Didn't they tell you they'd be out of town?"

"My secretary keeps track of all that," Grace said dismissively. "You'd think their niece's sweet sixteen would be important enough for them to make the effort. Or is your mother in one of her snits with me again?"

"I have no idea," Jen said, quite honestly.

Grace sighed. "Your mother has never spent a day of her life thinking of anyone but herself. Just look at the way she's neglected you over the years."

"Well, not everyone can be the wonderful mother that you are to Courtney," Jen said sarcastically.

Her jibe went right over her aunt's head. "Thank you, dear. Now, tell me why you felt you just had to wear that utterly inappropriate cocktail dress when you knew Courtney's party was formal."

"It's what I wanted to wear, Aunt Grace."

"Oh, Jennifer." Her aunt sighed. "I would have thought you'd outgrown it by now, but you still have this need to try and upstage my Courtney, you always have."

"No, Grace, I really don't. And I don't want to fight with you, either." She turned to Joey. "This is my friend, Joey Potter. Joey, this is my Aunt Grace."

"How nice of you to come," the older woman said.

"Thank you for having me," Joey replied.

"Can you excuse Jen for a little bit?" Grace asked, taking her niece's hand. "Her Uncle William is in the next room having cigars with his cronies, and he'll never forgive me if I don't bring in his favorite niece for a kiss."

"Sure," Joey said.

"Are you sure you're okay?" Jen asked.

"I'm fine," Joey assured her. "Go." Jen handed Joey her cider before she left with her aunt. Joey sipped it and watched them walk away, Jen's hand captive in her aunt's.

God, what a family, Joey thought, shuddering. And I thought *my* family was bad!

She looked around the room, recognizing some faces from the night before at The Cellar. The girl with the long red hair, Carson, waved to Joey from the dance floor. Joey waved back. Standing near the bar was the girl with the curly dark hair, what was her name? Amy something. She wore a long blue gown cut low in the back, and she was talking to Miranda the gossip queen.

Miranda and Amy looked over at Joey and caught her eye. Joey waved. They didn't wave back. Instead, Miranda leaned over and whispered something to Amy, then they both looked at Joey again.

Swell, Joey thought. Just like Capeside.

"Hi! Joey, isn't it?" A short, handsome guy stood next to her, grinning. "We met at The Cellar last night?"

"Right!" Joey said. She scrambled to try and come up with his name. "Chuck?"

"Tuck," he corrected her. "Tucker, actually. But everyone calls me Tuck."

"Sorry."

"Hey, it's fine," he said easily. "You got closer than most people. You look really beautiful."

"Thanks."

"This party is over the top, huh? Did you see that oil painting?"

"Who could miss it?" Joey asked.

Tuck laughed. So did Joey. "Great smile. It lights up your face. Would you like to dance?"

Joey hesitated. He was shorter than she was. Wouldn't it be kind of . . . awkward?

"I'm not great, but I think I can manage not to step on your feet."

He was just so sweet. "Sure," Joey said.

The orchestra was playing something slow and dreamy. Joey stood there self-consciously. Tuck put his arms around her. He didn't pull her close, the way Danny had. But he wasn't stiff, either. Actually, it was just fine. No fireworks. But fine.

She relaxed, as they moved to the music.

"Jen and I were in some classes together before she moved," Tuck said. "I always liked her. She's smart."

"She *is*," Joey agreed. "Everyone talks about how pretty she is, but they never talk about how smart she is."

"You guys are good friends, huh?"

Joey considered that for a moment. "We're . . . friends," she said cautiously. It was way too complicated to explain.

"Yo, Friar Tuck!" the tall guy dancing with Carson called from across the dance floor. "You're dancing! Psych!" His fist pumped the air.

"Friar Tuck?" Joey asked.

Tucker groaned. "I was an altar boy when I was a kid. And I do volunteer work at a Boy's Club. My friends think I live like a monk. I don't. But I want to hear about you."

"Like what?"

"Like I don't know. What's your dream?"

Joey looked at the dream ring on her finger. "My dream is to go to college. Ivy League, maybe, if I can ever get in. And to do something incredible with my life."

He smiled at her. "You will."

The music ended. As they applauded the orchestra, Miranda and Amy came over to them.

"Hey you two," Miranda chirped.

"Hi," Tuck said. He didn't sound thrilled to see her.

"Having fun, Joelle?" Amy asked.

"Sure," Joey replied.

"I just love your dress, Joelle," Miranda gushed. "It's so wonderfully tacky. Where did you get it, Chinatown?"

"Excuse me, was that supposed to be an insult?" Joey asked. "The reason I'm not sure is that it wasn't really clever enough to qualify."

"Oooh, dissed you, Miranda!" Amy hooted.

Miranda's eyes narrowed. "Very amusing."

"You ladies will excuse us, won't you?" Tuck asked. "We were just going to dance."

"Get over yourself, Tucker," Amy said, laughing. "You sound like your father!"

"We really only came over to ask you one question, Joelle," Miranda said.

Joey gave her a hard look. "Go for it."

"All right-y, then," Miranda said. "Is it true that you had sex with Danny Fields one hour after you met him?"

Chapter 16

Dawson and Pacey climbed up the subway stairs and began to walk toward the Plaza Hotel through the gently falling snow. They had dined on fast food, then cleaned up and changed clothes in the men's room back at Penn Station, being careful not to go anywhere near the newsstand run by the irate money-changer.

Under his ski parka, Dawson had on clean jeans, a denim shirt, and a tie. He carried his video camera under his arm. Pacey wore an old army fatigue jacket, the same jeans he'd worn since they'd left Capeside, and a clean, albeit extremely wrinkled, shirt.

"You really ought to lose the tie, dude," Pacey said, as they walked west toward Fifth Avenue. "Trying too hard is the kiss of death."

"I have other, more pressing concerns at the moment."

"Such as?" Pacey asked.

"Such as how can we just walk into a sweet six-teen party to which we were not invited? Such as what if Joey and Jen are not overjoyed at our unin-vited and unannounced presence?"

"See, Dawson, one of your many problems is that you worry too much. Go with the flow."

"That can be problematic if the flow is not flowing in the direction of your choice." The wind gusted, and Dawson zipped up his parka. "It occurs to me that I might be the dork of all time for chasing Joey to this party. I may need to rethink this."

"Fine," Pacey said, nodding. "Spend your life in your room, endlessly analyzing events and emotions that you are too weenie to actually live. Prove Joey right."

Dawson edged closer to the buildings to his right, trying to get out of the gusting wind. "Is that your attempt at reverse psychology, Pacey? In other words, am I supposed to want to crash this party because deep down I'm afraid that Joey was right, ergo, now I have this intense need to prove her wrong?"

"Basically, yeah," Pacey replied. "It's working beautifully, I might add."

They reached the Plaza Hotel, walked through the side entrance and entered the lavish lobby. The ceil-ing was high, the room lit by dangling crystal chan-deliers. The carpet under their feet was a rich tapestry, the furniture elegant. A string quartet played in an area to their left, where well-dressed couples sat having drinks. Everyone looked like they belonged to some exclusive club to which Pacey and Dawson would never be admitted.

"My stomach is registering somewhere between acute anxiety and overwhelming panic," Dawson managed, "and my mind is not far behind."

"Breathe, Dawson," Pacey instructed. "Follow my lead."

Pacey strolled over to the concierge's desk. "Good evening," he said, smiling unctuously at the gray-haired, uniformed gentleman.

"May I help you?" the concierge asked politely.

"Yes, you can," Pacey said. "We're the deejays from Bauhaus O'Funk."

The concierge looked at him blankly.

"Our equipment is out in the truck," Pacey continued. "We're doin' a little hamma-jamma thang at the sweet sixteen here this evening?"

"There's a sweet sixteen party in the Rose Room, one flight up," the concierge said. "But they have an orchestra, so I doubt that—"

"Hey, after midnight these things get wild and crazy," Pacey told him, winking. "Thanks. Stop on by later, when you get off. We'll throw a few Sinatra tunes on for you." He grabbed Dawson's arm and they headed for the elevator.

"Deejays from *Bauhaus O'Funk?*" Dawson's voice was withering.

"It's a sideline we should consider, actually," Pacey said. "Better pay than Screenplay. We wouldn't have to put up with Nellie. And deejays score all the hottest babes."

"Do you have any idea how demeaning to women it is when you talk like that?" Dawson asked.

"No," Pacey replied.

They got off the elevator and followed the brass sign directing them to the Rose Room.

And then, there they were. Staring in through the open doors.

It looked like a movie set. Everything female was in an evening gown, and everything male, including the orchestra and the waiters, was in a tux. It was beyond opulent. And way beyond them.

"Jack. Rose. *Titanic*. Ring any bells?" Pacey asked Dawson nervously.

"And you thought my *tie* was trying too hard," Dawson hissed at him. "We can't go in there!"

Pacey spied a pair of sunglasses someone had left on a white-clothed side table outside the Rose Room. He slid them on. "Dawson, we have not yet begun to party. Follow my lead."

"Pacey, no—"

Too late. Pacey bopped into the Rose Room, his eyes hidden behind the dark sunglasses.

Dawson caught up with him. "This is not *American Gigolo*. Lose the shades!"

"But—"

"I mean it, Pacey. Or I'm outta here."

Pacey reluctantly took off the sunglasses and stuck them in his back pocket. "You are soul-free, Dawson."

"Now go put the glasses back where you found them."

Pacey pointed at Dawson. "That sounded suspiciously like Deputy Doug. Not a good thing."

"Just do it," Dawson insisted.

Pacey sighed. "I shall return."

Dawson looked around. No sign of Joey or Jen. People stared at him, whispered, pointed. I look like a total goober, Dawson thought. He smiled and nodded to people.

A pretty girl with long red hair came up to him. "Hi."

"Hi."

"Are you sure you're at the right party?" she asked.

"I believe I am," Dawson said. Sweat began to pop out on his forehead, and he felt his armpits begin to drip sweat down his sides. He took off his ski parka.

"I'm Carson Finchworth. And you're—?"

"Dawson. Dawson Leery." She was staring at him as if she needed further explanation. "Deejay!" Dawson blurted out. "Bauhaus O'Funk!"

Carson laughed. "No way did Courtney's mom hire a deejay for this gig. She won't even let the orchestra play songs written in this decade. So who are you, really?"

"Really I'm . . ." Dawson looked down at the video camera in his hand. And it came to him. "I'm the videographer."

"Oh, cool!" Carson said. "So, you're gonna video the party? But didn't Grace tell you it was formal?"

"Grace?"

"Courtney's mom," Carson said. "Isn't she the one who hired you?"

"Screenplay Videos is a huge company," Dawson invented. "So they just send one of us videographers out."

"Mission accomplished," Pacey reported, as he

walked back over to Dawson. Then he noticed the cute redhead. "Hi there! I'm—"

"The other videographer," Dawson filled in. "I know I said they send one of us out. But in this case, they sent *two* of us. Because it's such a big party."

Carson gave Pacey a dubious look. "Where's your camera, hotshot?"

"I'm his boss," Pacey explained. "I direct. He does the actual grunt work."

"Uh-huh." She sounded highly dubious.

"Dawson, get some footage on this beauty," Pacey directed. He smiled at Carson. "Just look into the camera and tell Courtney whatever you want to tell her on her special day."

When this is all over, I really will kill Pacey, Dawson thought, as he aimed the camera at Carson. No jury of my peers would convict me, either.

"Why does every party hire you video guys?" Carson asked. "I look so fat on video. And I hate my voice!"

"You look great," Dawson insisted. "And your voice is cute. Just be yourself."

"Okay," Carson said. She looked into the camera self-consciously. "Happy sweet sixteen, Courtney. Your party is fantastic."

"See, you're a natural," Pacey told her. "I see Hollywood in your future, no lie."

Carson laughed. "Right. You are so full of it that I know why your eyes are brown."

"Hi, I'm Miranda," a small girl with pinched features said, coming over to them. "What are you guys doing?"

"They're the videographers," Carson said. "Say something for Courtney."

"Are Courtney's parents going to see this?" Miranda asked Dawson.

"Yes," Dawson said. "They hired me. I mean us. Our company. Screenplay Videos."

"Oh, too bad," Miranda said. "Then I don't dare say anything about how Courtney got so wrecked last weekend that she jumped in the hot tub naked with three guys."

"Is that true?" Carson asked, her jaw dropping open slightly.

"That's what I heard," Miranda said innocently. "Hey, you guys, come here!" she called to a group nearby. "We're making a tape for Courtney."

"Can you get all of us together?" one girl asked.

Dawson aimed the camera at them—three girls and two guys. They put their arms around each other.

"Happy birthday, Courtney," a tall guy said. "The party's rad, but kind of sedate. We'll have to do the alternate experience next weekend."

"No parents allowed!" a short girl added.

They all laughed, talking into the camera, fooling around, telling Courtney how much they loved her.

"You're groovin'!" Pacey whispered in Dawson's ear.

"Go see if you can find Joey and Jen," Dawson whispered back. "I didn't come here to make home videos."

"Excuse me." Someone tapped Dawson on the shoulder.

He turned around. A beautiful older woman in a dove-gray evening gown stood there.

Next to her was a middle-aged man in a tuxedo holding a video camera. On the man's left lapel was a plastic-enclosed badge that read "Sarrat Video Services, Joseph Sarrat, videographer."

"Hi," Dawson squeaked. His life passed before his eyes.

"I am the hostess of this party," the woman said. She pointed to the man next to her. "This gentleman is Joseph Sarrat, the videographer I engaged for this event. Now, you two have exactly twenty seconds to explain yourselves before I call hotel security."

Chapter 17

Joey checked the smoking room again. No Danny, just middle-aged men and a few women who thought it was cool, puffing on expensive cigars. She'd spent the past half hour looking for Danny. When she found him, she was going to force him to tell them all the truth. Or die trying.

But, after three trips around the massive ballroom and into the adjoining two suites, and even having checked out the other ballrooms on the hotel's second floor, she hadn't found him. Or Billy. Or even Jen, for that matter.

Joey plopped down on a buttery leather couch just outside of the ballroom. She felt that ache at the back of her throat that comes before tears, but willed them back.

This sucks, she thought. This really, really bites

it. All of Courtney's friends think I had sex with Danny. And Jen just deserted me.

"You okay, Joelle?" It was Tucker with two friends.

"Sure," Joey lied. Never let 'em see you sweat.

"Catch you later." Tucker went back into the Rose Room with his friends.

He doesn't want to know me anymore because he thinks I had sex with Danny, Joey thought. *Everyone* thinks I had sex with Danny.

She jumped up from the couch and made her way through the Rose Room to the coat check, where she'd left Jen's faux fur jacket. Forget it. She was not going to sit there and have a pity party for one. She'd just get a taxi back to Jen's apartment. Mrs. Richardson would let her in.

And then she remembered. She had spent her money on the dream ring. She didn't have enough left for a taxi.

The coat-check girl handed Joey the fur jacket. There was a small silver tray on the counter in front of her. Tips, Joey figured. She knew about people who lived on tips. She put one of her last two dollar bills on the tray. She'd be walking back to Jen's apartment anyway. It didn't make any difference.

"Joelle!"

She turned around. There was Danny, coming toward her in all his glory.

"I missed you," he said, his gait unsteady. Clearly he'd been either drinking or smoking pot or both. "I've been looking for you everywhere."

"And I've been looking for you, too," Joey said sweetly. "Want to hear something really weird? A lot of people at this party think I had sex with you last night."

"No kidding?" Danny asked, trying to laugh.

"No kidding. Miranda says you showed her some kind of chart where you rated my performance."

"Forget her. She's just jealous 'cuz she looks like a troll," Danny slurred. He reached for Joey but she stepped out of the way.

"You lied about me, didn't you." It was a statement, not a question. *"Didn't* you?"

He gave her a winsome little boy look that had clearly worked for him in the past. "Okay, Joelle, you busted me. But you wouldn't want me to ruin my rep by telling everyone you walked out on me, would you? Anyway, I made up for it tonight, right? And don't worry, I plan to keep on making up for it."

Joey grabbed the lapel of his tuxedo and yanked him to her. "You are a scum-sucking, bottom-feeding pile of puke. Your brain is in your pants, and it's a rice brain at that. Don't you ever, *ever* even breathe my name again as long as you live. If you see me on TV winning the Nobel Peace Prize, refer to me as 'that girl.' Because if I ever find out that my name has been uttered by your mouth—Joelle, Joey, Joe, take your pick—if I find out, and I *will* find out, I will make you so sorry."

She let go of him. He stumbled. She turned on her heel and headed for the door.

There was some commotion under way not far from the entrance to the Rose Room. A crowd of people was gathering to look at someone or something. Joey had zero interest. She was just about to walk by when she heard the ruckus.

"It's a perfectly innocent mistake! We were hired to video a different sweet sixteen!"

Joey jerked to a stop. No. It couldn't be.

That voice had sounded exactly like Pacey's.

"Right," another voice said. "We were hired to video . . . Courtney Giuliani's sweet sixteen."

Joey closed her eyes. She felt sick. Because there was absolutely, positively no mistaking that voice.

Dawson's voice. "This isn't happening," Joey moaned.

"We'll just wait for hotel security to straighten this all out, shall we?" Jen's aunt said frostily.

Joey worked her way through the crowd. There they were. Dawson and Pacey. In jeans. The eyes of the storm.

Dawson's gaze met hers. Then he looked quickly away. He was going to pretend he didn't know her, so he wouldn't risk getting her in trouble, too.

"Raymond, could you call security, please?" Courtney's mother asked one of Courtney's friends. She had one arm draped proprietarily around her daughter's shoulders.

"Don't do that," Joey said quickly.

Everyone turned to look at her. "I know these guys. I invited them."

"Wait, I don't understand," Courtney said. "You invited your friends to my sweet sixteen? I mean, I don't even know you."

"Danny knows her," someone smirked. There were a few muffled laughs.

"I guess you know lots of guys, huh, Joelle?" Miranda asked nastily.

"Shut up, Miranda," Carson said. "You're such a witch. No one can stand you!"

"Mother, my party is getting ruined!" Courtney wailed.

"Excuse me, excuse me," Jen said, muscling her way through the crowd. She desperately hoped she was wrong, but she could have sworn she'd heard the voices of Pacey and Dawson.

She reached the center of the commotion. She had been right. She was furious. Beyond furious. Her eyes met Dawson's. He looked like a deer caught in someone's headlights.

Attitude adjustment. Jen forced herself to smile. "Hi! You guys finally made it, huh?" She threw her arms around Dawson and hugged him, then she hugged Pacey.

"Jennifer?" her aunt asked in an icy voice.

"Oh, you know me, Aunt Grace," Jen said. "I invited these guys and forgot to tell you."

"You did this to ruin my party!" Courtney screeched.

"Honestly, Courtney, I—" Jen began.

"You haven't changed at all," Courtney accused, cutting her off. "Why don't you just get drunk and tear off your clothes, Jen, like old times?"

A few people gasped audibly. Jen flinched as if Courtney had hit her.

Dawson stepped forward and reached for Jen's hand. "I take full responsibility for this," he said. "Don't blame Jen or Joey. They didn't know we were coming. That's the truth. So I apologize,

Courtney. My friend and I will be leaving so that you can all get back to your party. That is, Courtney, just as soon as you apologize to Jen."

"You must be on drugs," Courtney spat. "I don't have to listen to you, and I certainly don't have to apologize to *her*. Mother, tell them!"

"Leave now or I am calling security," her mother said.

Pacey touched Dawson lightly on the shoulder. "Let's just go, pal."

"Not until she apologizes to Jen," Dawson insisted. He wouldn't move.

Someone else pushed through the crowd. Hotel security? No. It was Danny. His eyes lit up when he saw Joey and he reeled over to her. "Baby! You couldn't tear yourself away from me after all, huh, Joelle?"

"I told you never to say my name again," Joey told him. She pulled her fist back and let fly with a right cross that landed squarely on the left side of his nose. Hard. He lost his balance and fell over backward.

Everyone began to yell at once. Courtney's mother screamed for hotel security.

Joey looked at Jen, Dawson, and Pacey. "I think we know how this movie ends. Shall we?"

"We shall," Jen said.

The four of them walked out the door.

Chapter 18

By unspoken agreement they hurried out of the
hotel and jumped into one of the taxis waiting at
the curb, the guys and Joey in back, Jen in front.

The driver took off, heading down Fifth Avenue.
There was a beat of silence, then everyone but the
driver started yelling.

Jen and Joey both screamed at the guys for showing up without an invitation. The guys shouted back
their loud, if conflicting, explanations. Then Joey
turned her wrath on Jen, screaming at her for having
deserted her at the party.

"Time out, time out!" Jen yelled over the fray.
They didn't listen. She put two fingers in her mouth
and whistled shrilly. They stopped. The cabdriver
just kept his eyes on the road, as if screaming
matches in his taxicab were an everyday occurence.

"Thank you." She twisted around in her seat so

she could see them. "Now, if we speak one at a time, maybe we can make some sense of this. First let's deal with you and me, Joey, and then we can both deal with Dumb and Dumber."

"I resent that remark," Pacey said.

Jen shot him a disdainful glance. "If you value your life, Pacey, shut up." He mimed zipping his lips together.

Jen looked at Joey. "I know you think I abandoned you, but I didn't. After a few minutes of playing the dutiful niece to my Uncle William while he blew cigar smoke in my face, I went looking for Billy. When I found him, he and Jack D. had already gotten up close and personal. I got mad. We had a fight. I came back to look for you and you were gone. The end."

"I went looking for Danny," Joey said. "He told everyone that he . . ." Her gaze slid over to Dawson.

"He what?" Dawson demanded. Joey didn't reply.

"Is Danny the guy you punched?" Dawson asked, his voice tight. "Well? Is he?"

"None of your business," Joey snapped.

"As your best friend, it behooves me—"

"*Best friend?*" Joey echoed. Her eyes shot daggers at him. "You dare call me your *best friend?* Did it ever occur to that excuse for a brain you carry around between your ears that showing up at that particular party without an invitation was not exactly a *best friend* thing to do, Dawson? Because I'm just curious."

"You're the one who said I would spend my life in my room analyzing things to death instead of taking any chances," Dawson reminded her. "I believe

your exact taunt to me was, 'Be bold, Dawson.'
Well, I took a chance. I was bold. You just don't
like the chance I took."

"That is just your verbose and exceedingly lame
excuse for showing up at that party, Dawson! And
that is not exactly what I would put under the heading, 'bold.' "

"Were you with that guy Danny?" Dawson
asked doggedly.

"Yes, Dawson," Joey said sarcastically. "You see,
I deliberately punched out my own date. I *was* planning to run away with him after the party, but the
instant I saw you, I decided I just had to break his
nose instead."

"All right, I asked a stupid question," Dawson
allowed.

"The word 'pathetic' doesn't even begin to cover
you right now," Joey said, fuming.

"I just don't get it," Jen told Dawson and Pacey.
"I mean, what were you two thinking?"

"Road trip," Pacey said lamely.

Dawson could not let it go. "But if you *weren't*
on a date," Dawson continued, "then why did he
call you 'baby' and why did he—"

"I swear, Dawson, if you don't shut up I will hit
you a lot harder than I hit him!" Joey yelled.

"Please! No violence in my cab," the driver said,
looking at Joey in his rearview mirror.

"Fine," Joey said. "I'll wait until we get out."

The taxi pulled up in front of Jen's apartment
building. "You pay him," she told the guys. "Joey
and I will meet you in the lobby."

The two girls got out of the cab; Joey strode angrily into the building.

"I can't believe Dawson and Pacey," Joey said, pacing the lobby. "This is the lowest. Truly the lowest thing he has ever done to me." Then a vision of Danny lying on the ballroom floor filled her mind. Oh, god.

"And I can't believe I punched Danny out at your cousin's sweet sixteen," she added. She turned to Jen. Outside she could see the guys getting out of the taxicab. "Do you hate me?"

"Frankly, watching your fist connect with Danny Fields's face was one of the more satisfying moments of my life."

"But you wanted to change your rep with everyone, and then I . . . well, it couldn't have helped."

"I don't care what they think anymore, Joey," Jen said, "so forget it."

"Are you going to let Dawson and Pacey stay over?"

"Maybe they have a hotel room," Jen thought aloud.

"Dawson and Pacey? Hel-lo? What bank would they have robbed?" The guys came into the lobby. "How did you two even get to New York?" Joey asked them.

"My father's truck," Pacey said.

"We slept in it last night," Dawson added. "We had a detailed plan that involved calling you this morning, as opposed to springing our presence on you at the party. But do you know how many Lindleys there are in the Manhattan phone book?"

"Lots, none of them my parents. They're un-listed." Jen said. "So?"

"So we called them all!" Pacey held up his pointer finger. "I've got bursitis from punching numbers into the friggin' pay phone. Show a little pity."

Jen sighed. "I already regret what I'm about to do."

"You're about to offer us room at the inn, sustenance and shelter, I love you!" Pacey cried.

"Well, I don't love you," Jen stated matter-of-factly. "At the moment, I don't even like you. Either one of you."

They took the elevator to the penthouse floor.

"What about Mrs. Richardson?" Joey asked.

"What about her?" Jen let them into the dark apartment and turned on a light. Which was when the guys saw the abundance of flowers.

"Jen, you should be thinking float in the Tournament of Roses Parade," Pacey said, looking around.

Dawson nodded. "Quite the floral tribute."

"It so happens the flowers weren't for Jen," Joey said.

Dawson looked incredulous. *"You?"*

"What, is that so hard for you to believe?" Joey asked defiantly.

"No," Dawson said sadly. "I only wish I had sent them."

"What is going on here?" Mrs. Richardson was standing in the hallway. She held her modest flannel robe closed at the neck. Her hair stuck out in all directions.

"Some friends came back with us," Jen explained.

"Miss Lindley," the older woman began, "your

parents specifically forbid you to have male company here while they are away."

Jen walked over to her. "Look, these guys are from Capeside, and they don't have a place to sleep tonight."

"Capeside?" Mrs. Richardson asked dubiously.

"Where I live now," Jen replied. "So Joey and I are going to sleep in my bedroom. And my friends Dawson and Pacey are going to sleep in the guest room. That's the whole story. Nothing else. You can tell my parents I had two guys up here if that's what you need to do, Mrs. Richardson. They will have a fit and assume the worst about me, but what they assume won't be true. Now, even if all that happens, my friends are still going to spend the night. Because I don't turn away friends in need. So what's it going to be?"

The older woman fiddled with the collar of her robe. "I'm going to bed now, Miss Lindley," she finally said. "It's a pity I never woke up when you came in from your party this evening, but you see I took some allergy medicine and slept deeply through the night. Which means this conversation could not have even taken place. Good night."

She turned and left.

Jen smiled. "I knew I liked her."

"So, your parents are out of town, huh?" Pacey asked.

"I can see visions of strip poker dancing in your head, Pacey, but it's not gonna happen. You should be thrilled that I'm letting you stay at all." Jen looked over at Joey. "I'm beat."

"Me, too," Joey said.

"The guest room is second on the left," Jen told the guys. "Towels are in the guest bathroom. We can hash all this out tomorrow."

The girls headed out of the room.

"Joey, wait!" Dawson said. "We really need to talk—"

"No, Dawson. We really don't." She walked away.

A half hour later, the girls had changed into oversized T-shirts, shut the door, and climbed into Jen's huge bed. An old-fashioned orange night-light provided the only illumination.

"My right hand hurts," Joey confessed. "Do you think I might have busted his nose?"

"I hope so." Jen stared up at the ceiling. "I'm such an idiot. I never should have come back here. Did I really think my parents would magically be here to greet me with open arms? Or that my so-called friends would have changed? Or that Billy would be the answer to my problems?"

"What problems?" Joey asked softly.

"The usual adolescent angst of the overprivileged and underloved," Jen said. "I'm such a cliché that it's funny. All I want is someone to love me."

"I thought you told me you want friendship with a guy, not romance," Joey reminded her.

"I do. But my neediness ends up getting in the way of the friendship," Jen admitted. "So then I call it love—I even believe it's love!—because I want it to be true so badly. But I haven't ever had it, really. Not like you and Dawson."

"Dawson? We're *friends*," Joey insisted. "Not

that a friend would do what he just did. I am so ticked at him."

Jen got up on one elbow and peered at Joey. "How can you be so blind, Joey? You and Dawson are never going to be just friends again. He's in love with you and he always has been. And you're in love with him, too."

Joey sat up. "You're so full of it! I saw what you wrote on the wall in the girl's john at The Cellar. J + D. Jen and Dawson. You want him back. Why don't you just admit it?"

Jen laughed.

"What's so funny?" Joey asked crossly.

"You. J + D stood for Dawson and you!"

"I'm so sure."

"It did," Jen insisted. "You can't see what's right in front of your face. I don't want Dawson back, Joey. And I couldn't get him even if I did want him. He's your leading man, not mine."

"But I don't *want* him to be my leading man anymore!"

"What if we don't get endless chances at love, Joey?" Jen asked. "You wanted Dawson so badly. And then you got him. And then . . . then you just threw it away."

"You don't understand," Joey said, her voice low. "You're this sophisticated New Yorker. You've dated lots of guys. But I'm from Capeside and Dawson Leery is the only guy I've ever known. How am I supposed to know if he's the one for me when I haven't even lived yet?"

"Maybe you aren't," Jen allowed. "But don't fault

him for loving you, Joey. Love is too precious and rare to throw away. Trust me, I know."

After a while, Joey heard Jen's breathing deepen, and she knew Jen was asleep. She just lay there with her eyes closed, watching the geometric patterns and lights playing on the insides of her eyelids. But she couldn't sleep. She was thinking. Finally she got up and padded down the hall to the room where Dawson and Pacey were asleep.

She opened the door slowly, so that a shaft of light fell on Dawson's bed.

His wide-open eyes met hers. As if he could read her mind, he got out of bed and followed her, wordlessly, into the living room.

"I couldn't sleep," she said finally, as she stood by the living room window facing Dawson, the lights of Manhattan silhouetting her from behind.

"Me, neither."

They sat down together on the couch, in the dark. He had on gym shorts and a T-shirt. Joey pulled the hem of her long T-shirt even longer, and tried to find the words she wanted to say.

"Remember last fall, Dawson? We had one of our revoltingly intense, pseudo-mature conversations about honesty. And I told you it was time for you to grow up and be honest with me. Remember?"

Dawson nodded.

"Well, I wasn't exactly honest with you tonight. The truth is . . . I was on a date with Danny. That is, I agreed to go to the party with him. I met him Friday night with Jen. It was all very Julie Delpy and Ethan Hawke, you know, strangers who see each other and feel this intense spark—"

Like I felt with Dixie, Dawson thought. No. That was different. That was real.

"—And this intense spark feels so awesome, so special—"

"I don't want to hear about your sparks with another guy, Joey."

"You have no choice, Dawson. So, this girl and this guy have this intense spark," she went on. "Only it turns out that, beyond the hormonal, the spark was an illusion. Because all he was interested in was sex. And when he didn't get it, he lied and told everyone that he had."

Dawson's throat ached. "I don't know what to say to that, Joey. I don't know what role to play now. The avenging boyfriend? The distant ex-boyfriend? The understanding friend?"

Joey got up and went to the window again. The lights of New York beckoned seductively. Was it just the night before that the skyline had called to her so sweetly? Jen had been right. Everything that glittered was not gold.

"I can't tell you what role to play," she said, still staring out at the glittering lights. "All I know is that I wanted to tell you the truth."

She slowly turned to him. "Dawson, I don't know if you can understand because I don't even understand it myself. When it comes to guys I'm still in the infant stage. I have a lot of learning to do, and I'll probably make a lot of mistakes along the way."

She waited. He was silent. Impassive.

"So I can't tell you that I want more than your friendship right now," she continued, "because it would be a lie. But I can tell you that even though

I'm incredibly ticked at you for following me to New York, I value your love and your friendship more than anything in the world. If I lost it, I don't know what I would do. So I just wanted you to know."

Silence.

She went back to the couch and sat down. She looked into his eyes. "Dawson? Could you please say something?"

Their faces were so close that he could smell the mint of her toothpaste. And something else, something uniquely and sweetly Joey. He longed to kiss her. And knew he couldn't. Shouldn't. Wouldn't.

"Dawson?"

He stood up. Avoid temptation. Don't think. Don't feel. "Thanks for being honest with me."

She stood up, too. "Is that *it*?"

"What do you want me to say? That I understand? That in the future you can feel free to come to me to expound on your burgeoning love life? Because I can't say that." He walked to the door. Then he turned back to her.

"For once you don't get the stinging exit line, Joey. I do. But for the life of me, I can't remember what it is."

Chapter 19

Jen rested her head on the truck passenger window, her mood as gloomy as the gathering clouds. She'd been awakened that morning by a phone call. Aunt Grace. Her aunt yelled at her hysterically for ten minutes. The party had been ruined. Danny had spent hours in the emergency room—yes, his nose was broken—and it was all Jen's fault for bringing that white-trash girl with her.

"Jennifer Lindley, you'll be a pregnant, alcoholic drug addict before you're a senior in high school," her aunt had predicted. "And you won't even know who the baby's father is."

"Aunt Grace?" Jen had finally interrupted.

"What?" her aunt asked.

"Go to hell." Jen hung up on her. Click.

Almost instantly, the phone had rung again. Billy. Everything that had gone wrong had been his fault.

He loved her. He wanted her back. Couldn't he see her before she went back to Capeside? In fact, why did she have to go back to Capeside at all?

She didn't hang up on him, as she had on her aunt. All she'd said was "I have to go, Billy. I need some time alone. I'll call you when I call you." Click. Disconnect. From him, from her entire life in New York.

"According to my calculations," Pacey said, as he switched lanes to pass a Taurus, "I will have this truck back in the Chief of Police's parking spot exactly one hour before he hits Capeside. He'll never know it was gone."

"Maybe I'll tell him," Joey said. "You deserve it."

"There are things that I believe you would do to me, Joey," Pacey said, "many of them most unpleasant. But ratting me out to my father is not one of them. Besides, you're going home in the lap of luxury."

Joey was squished between Pacey and Dawson on the cab's single seat. Jen was curled up behind them.

"Very amusing," Joey retorted. "On the big score-card of life, you and Dawson are batting zero for this little stunt. No. *Sub*-zero. You will have to do something amazing, like, say, cure cancer, to *rise* to zero. A free ride home in a stolen truck does not qualify."

"Okay, you're still mad," Pacey allowed, as he switched back to the right-hand lane.

Joey stretched and almost elbowed Dawson in the nose. "Aren't you the mental giant, Pacey. How could I have missed such burning intellect?" Ragging on Pacey was so much easier than thinking about Dawson. Or even *looking* at Dawson. It was bad enough sitting pressed against him like this, even if he was studiously ignoring her.

"Consider adopting Jen's approach to anger," Pacey suggested, looking at Jen in the mirror. "Sure, she's not altogether happy. Yet her deep affection for us is untarnished. Plus, her pensive silence is much easier on the eardrums."

"Think again, Pacey," Jen said. "Joey's the bad cop and I'm the good cop. Don't be fooled into thinking we aren't on the same side."

"Meaning that your deep affection for us *is* tarnished?" Pacey asked, sounding surprisingly vulnerable.

"What do you think?" Jen asked. "In some parallel universe you might do something this idiotic and your friends would still give you the unconditional love that your family seems incapable of giving, but you don't live in that universe, Pacey. And neither do I."

It began to rain, which seemed fitting. For a long time, no one said anything.

"Your father will know about the truck," Jen finally said. "The odometer."

"He and my brother are oblivious to that stuff," Pacey said. "Too busy combatting Capeside's many serial killers. I had a new run-in with Deputy Doug last week. He waited up for me when I came in late just so he could tell me one more time what a loser I am."

"Fast-forward," Joey snapped. "Been-there-done-that."

Pacey nodded. "Okay, one whine over the pity

line. But you know what? Even if I woke up tomorrow as Deputy Doug the second, in everyone's eyes I'd still be Pacey-the-loser. Because once people think they have you pegged, they never change their opinion of you. Right, Jen?"

Jen didn't answer.

"Right," Pacey said. "But someday I'll escape from Capeside, just like you escaped from New York. And when I do, I too will reinvent myself. But in the meantime, a road trip to New York was as close as I'm gonna get."

Joey looked back at Jen. "This is where we gain the insight that elicits newfound sympathy for a previously unsympathetic character."

Pacey just shook his head. "Thanks, Joe. Your compassion runneth over."

"Just a word of advice," Joey said. "Resist the temptation to have your character tell us how he feels, instead of allowing us to discover it for ourselves."

"Forget it," Pacey mumbled with disgust. He turned the radio on, loud.

Dawson cut his eyes at Joey. He knew her too well—her inverse relationship between happiness and verbosity. Meaning that if she was on a verbal roll, she was probably miserable.

But not over me, he realized. What kind of mental meltdown made me think she'd welcome my presence in New York? She wants to see other guys. And no brilliant turn of phrase or impetuous, romantic trip to New York is going to get her to change her mind.

A movie moment in his head: a graceful girl, with

long blond hair, dancing in the parking lot of Mc-
Donald's. Dixie. If he was with Dixie, she'd appreci-
ate him. She'd—

"Look at the poor woman!" Jen said.

Off in the distance, on the shoulder of the road,
a small elderly woman stood in the downpour, looking helplessly at her blown left tire. Cars whizzed
by her.

Pacey quickly checked his watch. Time to spare
without risking the wrath of the Long Arm of the
Law. He slowed down and pulled the truck off the
highway, right behind the woman's Lexus.

"This is where you get out of the truck and actually go *help* her," Jen pointed out.

"I'm going, I'm going," Pacey said. He watched
the highway hopefully. "That is, if some other Good
Samaritan with an *umbrella* doesn't pull off to help
her first."

Jen nudged him in the back. "You won't melt."

"Oh, *that's* original," Pacey said.

Dawson unlocked his door. "Come on."

Dawson and Pacey ran to the woman, the rain
soaking them. "Hi!" Dawson said. "Can we help
you?"

"Bless you for stopping," the woman said. "I'm
such a ninny. I forgot my cell phone and I'm hope-
less about cars."

Pacey knelt down to look at the left rear tire of
her Lexus. "Your basic blown tire."

"Yes, I can see that," the woman said. "I have a
spare and a jack." She unlocked the trunk and
Dawson and Pacey lifted out the tire and the jack.

"We can put the spare on for you," Pacey offered.

"You're a lifesaver," she said gratefully. "My name is Phyllis Hanover, by the way."

The boys introduced themselves to her.

"Wait in our truck if you'd like," Dawson suggested. "No sense in your standing in the rain."

"I will," Mrs. Hanover said. "I simply can't thank you enough for this." She made her way to the truck and got in.

Dawson stared at Pacey, the rain pelting down on him. "Now what?"

"What do you mean 'now what?' " Pacey asked. "Don't you know how to change a tire, Dawson?"

"I'm sure I will learn how to change a tire in the near future," Dawson said, "but—"

"Get Joey," Pacey said, shaking his head. "Go! I'm in a time crunch, here!"

Dawson went back to the truck. Joey came out. Wordlessly she grabbed the jack and wedged it in place while Pacey got down and loosened the lug nuts and bolts. Then, she jacked the car up.

"Thanks for your help," Pacey said.

"I'm not helping *you*," Joey said. "I'm helping *her*. Where's the spare?"

"Here."

Inside the truck, the older woman dried her curly gray hair with some paper towels Jen had found in the cargo space. "I just don't know what I would have done if you young people hadn't stopped."

"We're glad we could help," Jen said.

"It's amazing how rarely people help each other anymore. It's a pity. The world is a poorer place for it. What did that young man say his name was again?"

"Pacey Witter," Dawson told her.

"Unusual name, Pacey," Mrs. Hanover said. "Where do you children live?"

"Capeside," Jen said. "Actually, Pacey's dad is the Chief of Police there."

"Capeside, Capeside," the woman mused. "I don't believe I've heard of it. We summer in Martha's Vineyard. Is it near there?"

Jen laughed. "It's light-years from there."

The door opened. Joey got into the driver's seat as Pacey stood in the downpour.

"Listen, Mrs. Hanover, your spare tire is flat," Joey said.

"Oh, no!"

"Oh, yes," Joey said, shivering as the water dripped off of her. Wordlessly Dawson helped her off with her jacket. Then he took off his ski parka and put it around her shoulders.

"We'll have to find a service station that can bring you out a tire or get one of yours fixed," Pacey said. He looked around. "We're not near anything. It's Sunday. It could take a while."

"No, wait," Jen said. "There are emergency call boxes on this highway every mile. We've been passing them."

"I'll go see if I can find one," Pacey said.

"I hate to trouble you," Mrs. Hanover replied.

Pacey quickly glanced at his watch. If he cut loose from this little mission of mercy within the next thirty minutes, they were still home-free.

"Well, it's not exactly a *cure for cancer*," he intoned, looking at Joey pointedly, "but it's no trouble."

164

"Look Pacey," Joey shivered slightly as she talked. "Why don't you throw Mrs. Hanover's spare in the back of the truck and go see if you can get some help. Go to the call box, or maybe there's a gas station that's open."

"Good idea," Pacey said, glancing at his watch again.

"I'll go too," Jen said suddenly.

"But why?" Dawson asked. "You can wait in Mrs. Hanover's car with Joey and me."

"Frankly, Dawson, I don't think you want Joey and me both with you right now. That much anger aimed in your direction might be too much anger for you to deal with."

Dawson nodded. He and Joey got out of the truck and went to Mrs. Hanover's car. Pacey threw the spare tire in the back of the truck. Then, he, Jen, and Mrs. Hanover headed down the road.

In the front seat of Mrs. Hanover's car, Joey shivered and watched Pacey's truck disappear down the highway.

"They'll be back soon," Dawson said.

Joey started the car so she could turn on the heater. Warm air blew from the vents.

Dawson's eyes slid over to Joey. "You're still shivering," he noted.

"That might be because I'm still freezing."

"What I'm about to do is meaningless beyond a human desire to raise your body temperature." Dawson put his arm around her. "In a nonsexual way, I should add," he said hastily.

"Got that, Dawson. Thanks."

They sat in silence.

"Who said 'Timing is everything'?" Dawson asked.

Joey shrugged. "Fred Astaire? The Unabomber?"

Dawson stared straight ahead, watching rain pelt the windshield. "I'm sitting here with you, my best friend, and what I want to do is tell you all about this magical girl I can't stop thinking about. How her hair curls up around her face when it gets wet. How her eyes change with every emotion she feels. How no one could possibly understand her the way that I can. But I can't tell you about her, Joey, because you *are* her. So that's what I mean about timing. Ours is decidedly off. And I just don't know what to do about it or how to fix it."

"It's not a movie, Dawson. You can't fix it."

They sat in silence again. Minutes passed. A half hour. They both fell asleep. When they woke up, they realized they had been there more than an hour.

"Pacey's schedule has been drastically altered," Dawson said, stretching. "He must be going crazy."

Joey shrugged. "Here's what happened. They found a call box and called the state police. The state police said that with this weather and it being Sunday, all the wreckers were busy. But if they'd drive three exits north, they'd find a service station that could help them. And that's where they are now."

"Do you run a psychic service you neglected to mention to me?" Dawson asked.

"When you ride with Bessie in her bomber, you know everything that can go wrong in a car," Jen said. "And you know where every service station in this part of Massachusetts is located."

"Pacey's father is going to kill him," Dawson said.

"Amazing," Joey said. "Pacey Witter refused to leave Grandma Moses deserted by the side of the road. This is like discovering the eighth wonder of the world."

Dawson nodded. "Just when you think you can trust someone to always do the wrong thing, Pacey goes and does the right thing. It's a little off-putting."

"A miracle on the road to Capeside. An amazing moment. Pacey transcends self-involved stupidity." She gave Dawson a dry look. "Who knows, Dawson, maybe it'll be contagious."

Chapter 20

"*J*ennifer? Is that you?" Jen's grandmother came out of the kitchen, wiping her hands on her apron.

"Hi, Grams." Jen put down her suitcase and hung her sopping-wet leather jacket in the hall closet.

"I thought you were going to call me from the train station, Jennifer."

"We got a ride."

"I see. Well. It's funny. I found myself rather missing your company. I know you find that hard to believe."

"I do," Jen agreed. "Because most of the time I'm not very good company to you, and we both know it."

"Did you have a good time?"

"Swell," Jen said. "Any calls for me?"

"Just one from Clifford Elliot," Grams said. "I left his number by the phone. How was Courtney's sweet sixteen?"

"The word 'unforgettable' comes to mind."

"Really?" Grams asked, her face lighting up. "I'd love to hear about it."

"Some other time," Jen said. "I've got a splitting headache."

Grams' face fell. "I see."

Jen picked up her suitcase. "I'm beat. I'm going to bed." She headed upstairs.

"What about dinner?" Grams called after her. "I prepared some of your favorite things."

"Thanks, I'm not hungry."

She went up to her room, changed into her favorite nightgown, and crawled into bed.

A terrible loneliness swept over her. It was time to face the truth. She didn't belong in New York anymore. Everyone back there thought they knew her, but they really didn't know her at all. And even worse, they didn't care about her. Not really.

Pretend affection is the worst, Jen thought. I would rather have no affection at all. Except that no affection is just so lonely.

A single tear slid down her cheek and she fisted it away. The odor of roast chicken wafted up the stairs. Her stomach growled hungrily. It was sweet of Grams to make roast chicken and to say she missed me. But I can't talk to her. If only Gramps was still alive. . . .

"But he isn't," she said aloud, as if it would help her to accept it. "He isn't, and she is. And that is just the way it is."

From downstairs, Jen heard her grandmother singing a church hymn. They came from two different planets. There were all kinds of things about her life that she could never tell Grams, because she'd never understand. But at least Grams was there for her, which was more than she could say for her parents. And her friends in Capeside were there for her, too, which was more than she could say for her so-called friends in New York.

Jen got out of bed, padded downstairs, and went into the kitchen. Her grandmother was in the process of taking away one table setting.

"Can I join you?" Jen asked.

Grams turned around. She took in Jen's long nightgown. "Not unless you dress properly for the table."

"Do you think just this once we could dispense with the rules, Grams? I thought we could have a nice dinner together. And I could tell you about the sweet sixteen."

Grams pressed her lips together, but put the second plate back on the table. "All right. Yes."

They sat down, and Grams said grace. Jen put a napkin on her lap and reached for the mashed potatoes. "Well, Grams, you wanted to hear about the party. It was fantastic," she began. "It was held in the most exquisite ballroom. There was an orchestra. And dancing."

"How lovely," Grams said happily, and passed the platter of chicken to Jen. "Ballroom dancing."

"And let me tell you about this oil painting of Courtney her mother had done . . ."

Jen went on and on, painting a beautiful picture of a fantasy party. As for the tawdry truth, *that* she could hash over with Joey. What a weird thought.

Were they going to be, well, friends?

* * *

Dawson walked in the house. His parents were watching television. They clicked it off immediately.

"Hi," he said.

"How was your weekend *at Pacey's?*" his father asked.

Dawson could tell from the tone of his father's voice that he was in major trouble. Chief Witter must have already called them.

Dawson sat down. "Mom, Dad, I lied to you. You know I wasn't at Pacey's for the weekend."

"You were in Albany at some rock concert," his mother said. "We've known that since yesterday when Doug Witter called us. He said the police were going to press charges against Pacey for stealing the truck."

Dawson shook his head as if to clear it. *"What?"*

"Someone told Doug where you guys were," Mitch said. "We've been frantic, Dawson. We had no way to track you down, no way to get—"

"Dad, we weren't anywhere near Albany."

"You weren't?" Gale asked. "Where were you then?"

"New York."

"City?" his mother asked incredulously.

Dawson nodded. "Joey went there with Jen for the weekend. We sort of . . . we decided to . . . join them."

"Follow them, you mean?" his father asked. "You took Witter's truck and followed Jen and Joey to New York? Have you completely taken leave of your senses?"

"That's one possible explanation," Dawson agreed.

Gale shook her head. "I just don't know what to

say to you, Dawson. Can you even imagine how worried we've been?"

"Now I can. But I didn't know that you knew. And what you knew wasn't the truth." He looked from his mom to his dad. They had never looked at him like that before. Like he had disappointed them. Let them down.

"I used poor judgment," Dawson added.

"This is much bigger than 'poor judgment,'" his father said. "Poor judgment is coming in a half hour after curfew. Poor judgment is a beer at a party. Dawson, we've always trusted you. And until now, you've never given us a reason not to."

"I'm sorry," Dawson said. "If I could do a total rewrite on this past weekend, believe me, I would."

Mitch sighed. "Well, your mom and I agree that we have to punish you for this. Grounding you is pointless. Everything you love is up in your room."

Not quite everything, Dawson thought.

"So we've decided to take away your VCR and your video camera for two weeks," his mother said.

"But I need my camera for film class!" Dawson cried.

"You should have thought of that before you pulled this stupid stunt," Mitch said. He turned to his wife. "Oh my god, I sounded exactly like my father just now. Scary."

Dawson got up. "All right. I accept my punishment. And while I could tell you that I'll never do anything this stupid again, the odds are that, as a teenager on the brink of adulthood, I will."

"I imagine that's so, Dawson," his father said.

"And your mom and I will be right here to kick your butt for it."

Dawson nodded. For some bizarre reason, the idea didn't upset him all that much. In fact, it didn't really upset him at all.

Even walking up to the house, Joey could hear the baby's colicky howls. She briefly considered turning around and rowing back over to Dawson's house. But she knew she couldn't do that. So she went inside.

Man, that kid has a set of lungs. Joey dropped her backpack in the living room. It was a mess. A bottle leaking milk lay on the battered coffee table. There was a pile of Pampers next to a mucky-looking teething ring. The carpet was littered with zwieback crumbs.

Home, sweet home.

Bessie came into the living room, the baby wailing in her arms. "Shhhhh," she crooned to him. "Poor little guy. Please stop crying." She looked up and saw Joey. "Thank God you're back." She made a beeline for her sister and dumped the baby into her arms.

"I have had to pee for the past hour but I didn't want to put him down." She hurried to the bathroom.

Alexander upped his decibel level. He was wet. He smelled like sour milk. "What's wrong with him?" Joey yelled to her sister.

"Teething!" Bessie called back. "The doctor told me it's normal. What the hell do I know?"

Joey sat on the couch with the infant. Something

stuck into her butt. She pulled it out. A rattle. She shook it at the baby. He swatted it away and kept crying.

This will never, ever be my life, she vowed, rocking the screaming baby in her arms. I will never get stuck with a baby and no money and no way out. And I will never get stuck in Capeside.

Bessie came back from the bathroom and sat next to Joey. The baby cried frantically and grabbed for her. She took him, rocked him, but it was futile. "I'm losing my mind here, Joey."

"Well, you picked it," Joey snapped before she could stop herself.

"What's that supposed to mean?"

"It means who told you to have a baby if you weren't ready to take care of a baby?" Joey asked.

"Some things just happen, Joey," Bessie said, an edge to her voice. "Look, can you take him for five minutes? Maybe change him? I need to call the restaurant." She didn't wait for an answer, and thrust Alexander at Joey.

"No!" Joey jumped up, ignoring Bessie's outstretched arms. "I don't want to take him. He's your responsibility, not mine. You had him, not me. So just deal with it!" Joey picked up her backpack and headed for her room.

"You give new meaning to the word 'selfish,' Joey!"

Joey wheeled around. "Me? How about a 'Welcome home, Joey.' Or 'Did you have fun, Joey?' But no. I walk right back into the same crap that was here when I left."

"Because I covered for your absent butt so you

could leave!" Bessie exclaimed. "I didn't mind, Joey. I was happy, because it was actually something that I could do for you. But forgive me if the world didn't stop while you were away. Contrary to what you think, it does not revolve around you."

"Nice, Bessie. Very Joan Crawford. I understand her kids screamed a lot, too." Joey stomped out of the room, went into her bedroom, and slammed the door so hard the whole house shook.

Pacey sat in the living room facing his father. He'd been shocked to find out that Deputy Doug had come home from the convention early and somehow had heard that Pacey and Dawson had gone to the Nightshade concert in Albany.

Not that it made any sense, but it did mean that all the time he'd been sweating it, playing Dudley Do-right to Mrs. Hanover, waiting for the service station to repair her spare tire, he was already in doo-doo of the deepest sort.

There was a certain irony to it that, if his father hadn't been about to kill him, Pacey might have even appreciated.

"If you and Dawson were not in Albany, Pacey," his father asked in measured tones, "then where were you?"

"New York City," Pacey replied. "To see friends."

"You stole my truck and went to New York to see friends," his father repeated.

"I don't supposed you'd consider plea-bargaining it down to 'borrowed'?" Pacey ventured.

His father leaned forward on the couch. "You

have no idea how close you came to spending tonight in my jail."

Pacey smiled. "You wouldn't do that."

"Damn straight I'd do that," his father said. "I probably should have. You're out of control, Pacey. The sad thing is, you think it's funny. It's all a big joke to you. I'm ashamed to call you my son."

There it was. That swift, lethal pain as the knife went in.

"Look, I messed up," Pacey admitted. "Can we just move on to the sentencing phase?"

His father's face mottled with anger. "Look at you. You've never done a decent thing in your life. You don't care about anyone but yourself. You made your own bed, Pacey. Now you can damn well lie in it. You know, there's a program for juvenile offenders in Utah—"

"Wait, wait," Pacey interrupted. "You can't be serious."

"As a heart attack. You're still subject to arrest for stealing my truck. And that's exactly what I intend to do."

"This scene would benefit from rewrites," Pacey said. His heart was hammering in his chest.

"I have nothing to say to you anymore, Pacey. I wash my hands of you."

Mr. Witter got up and went to the phone. But before he could place a call, it rang. He picked it up. "Chief Witter speaking," he said.

"Chief Witter," a cultured female voice said. "You don't know me. My name is Phyllis Hanover. I'm a retired county clerk. I live in Andover. I must speak with you about your son, Pacey."

Mr. Witter shook his head. "What did he do now, ma'am?"

"Well, he was wonderful, Chief Witter," the woman said. "My tire blew on the interstate this afternoon. Not only did your son stop to help me, he insisted on taking me to a service station that would repair it, and he didn't leave me until I was back on the road."

"Are you sure you're talking about my son?" Mr. Witter asked. "Pacey Witter?"

"I'm absolutely certain," the woman said. "I offered him a reward but he refused to take anything from me. So I just felt I had to look up your number and call you, to let you know what a truly remarkable son you have raised. You should be very proud of him, Mr. Witter."

"Yes, ma'am," Mr. Witter said. "Thanks for calling." He hung up and turned to Pacey. "That was a woman by the name of Phyllis Hanover. She met you this afternoon?"

"She did."

"She says you spent hours today helping her after she lost a tire."

"I was there," Pacey agreed.

"Why didn't you tell me about it?" Mr. Witter asked.

Pacey looked confused. "When? When you said you were ashamed I was your son? Or when you told me you were having me arrested?"

His father shook his head sadly and walked heavily from the room.

Pacey hurried after him. "Might I assume that my arrest is not imminent?"

His father didn't turn around. "No arrest, Pacey."

"And no Utah boot camp thing?"

"No Utah," his father said. Now he turned to his son. "I'll ground you just like I always ground you. You'll stay home for a while and then you'll weasel out of it until the next time. For the life of me, Pacey, I will never understand what makes you tick."

"That makes two of us, Dad," Pacey said. "That makes two of us."

Joey took the pillow off her head. She listened carefully. Could it be true? Yes! Alexander had finally stopped crying! She tiptoed into the living room, knowing from experience that any noise would wake the kid up again.

Her sister and the baby were asleep on the couch, the baby in Bessie's arms. Bessie looked like a wreck. Tired. Old. Worn out. It tore at Joey's heart. What had happened to her cool sister? When had she given up on her dreams?

When Mom died, Joey thought. She thought she had to be my mom. And her own mom. And now Alexander's mom, too.

Joey began to clean up some of the mess on the coffee table. At least when Bessie woke up it would be a little neater. The ring she'd bought in New York, now on her forefinger, caught her eye. The sun, the moon, and the stars. A dream ring, the artist had called it.

Joey pulled it off. Then she slowly, carefully, slipped it into Bessie's right hand. "I brought you something back from New York, Bessie," she whispered. "Sweet dreams."

She took the phone to her bedroom and punched in Dawson's number.

"Hello?" he answered.

"I see your parents allowed you to live," she said.

"They implied it might be temporary," Dawson replied.

"Isn't everything?" Joey asked. "I just called to say good night, Dawson. No clever exit lines. I know I should have one for every occasion and I'm a little disappointed in myself for being so unprepared but there you are. I won't be climbing in your window tonight. But I did want to hear the sound of your voice."

"Joey?"

"What?"

"Nothing. Just Joey."

"I haven't changed my mind about anything, Dawson. You need to know that."

"I know that. Joey?"

"What?"

"There's something I didn't tell you about this weekend," Dawson said. "I met a girl. A ballet dancer named Dixie. And even though I only knew her for the briefest time, something about her touched me."

"Why are you telling me this, Dawson?"

"You asked me to be honest," Dawson told her. "You were honest with me."

"Are you going to see this girl again?"

"I don't even know her last name," Dawson admitted. "And I realize that if I did get to know her,

179

the reality of her might be nothing at all like my fantasy. I suppose I could simply be making her into what I want her to be. A new romantic heroine for Dawson. But for five minutes there, I felt like anything was possible."

A tenderness clutched Joey's heart. "Dawson?" she whispered.

"What?"

"Nothing," Joey said, smiling. "Just Dawson."

About the Creator/Executive Producer

Born in New Bern, North Carolina, Kevin Williamson studied theater and film at East Carolina University before moving to New York to pursue an acting career. He relocated to Los Angeles and took a job as an assistant to a music video director. Eventually deciding to explore his gift for storytelling, Williamson took an extension course in screenwriting at UCLA (University of California, Los Angeles).

Kevin Williamson has experienced incredible success in the film medium. His first feature film was *Scream*, directed by Wes Craven and starring Drew Barrymore, Courteney Cox, and Neve Campbell. He has also written other feature films including the psychological thriller *I Know What You Did Last Summer*, based on the Lois Duncan novel, and directed by Jim Gillespie. His first foray into television, *Dawson's Creek*™, has already received high praise from television critics for its honest portrayal of teen life.

About the Author

C. J. Anders is the pseudonym for a well-known young-adult fiction-writing couple.

Read more about Joey, Dawson, Pacey, and Jen in these four new, original Dawson's Creek™ stories.

Long Hot Summer
Calm Before the Storm
Shifting Into Overdrive
Major Meltdown*

And don't miss:

DAWSON'S CREEK
The Official Postcard Book

DAWSON'S CREEK
The Official Scrapbook

Available now from Pocket Books

*coming soon

2041